A Candlelight Ecstasy Romance ®

"I'M INTERESTED IN YOU, KYLIE. AS A WOMAN, NOT AS A PROFESSIONAL."

An insult rolled inside a compliment, it annoyed her out of all proportion. "Oh, I see," she said. "Maybe I should approach this problem from another angle. Would you prefer that I persuade you with a few feminine wiles to honor my contract?"

"Kylie," Nick said with quiet warning. "You know that isn't what I—"

"Suppose I make you an offer you can't refuse. I probably should have changed tactics sooner, but I gave you credit for being more professional. Silly of me, wasn't it? If I'd known that all I had to do to get this job was stroke your ego and . . ."

The sentence trailed off suggestively. In some distant corner of her mind, Kylie was shocked at her own audacity, but she couldn't seem to stop. Her hands pressed against his chest as she raised her lips to rest intimately against his, shocked at the searing response of his touch.

A CANDLELIGHT ECSTASY ROMANCE ®

WINDS OF
HEAVEN

Karen Whittenburg

A CANDLELIGHT ECSTASY ROMANCE ®

For Michael, because . . .
And for Jill and Paul, with love

To Our Readers:

We have been delighted with your enthusiastic response to Candlelight Ecstasy Romances®, and we thank you for the interest you have shown in this exciting series.

In the upcoming months we will continue to present the distinctive sensuous love stories you have come to expect only from Ecstasy. We look forward to bringing you many more books from your favorite authors and also the very finest work from new authors of contemporary romantic fiction.

As always, we are striving to present the unique, absorbing love stories that you enjoy most—books that are more than ordinary romance.

Your suggestions and comments are always welcome. Please write to us at the address below.

Sincerely,

The Editors
Candlelight Romances
1 Dag Hammarskjold Plaza
New York, New York 10017

CHAPTER ONE

The touch on her arm was firm and definitely masculine. Kylie Richards turned and glanced at the well-shaped hand, noting the suggestion of strength in the long fingers. Her brows lifted in polite question as her gaze followed the length of tanned, muscled forearm to a short-sleeved yellow shirt that covered but didn't conceal a powerful chest and shoulders.

"Excuse me." His voice was deep with a pleasant resonance, easily heard even in the noisy surroundings of the small Santa Fe airport. "Do you need some help with your luggage?"

Kylie looked past a strong chin, a pair of lips just beginning to tip upward at the corners, a slightly arrogant nose, and found herself staring into gray eyes, glinting with silvery humor.

She had a fleeting sense of recognition and then realized he had sat a few seats in front of her on the plane. Memory quickly provided sketchy details: the way he'd greeted one of the flight crew and been greeted in return as a frequent and valued passenger; the way he'd walked with such authority to the one remaining vacant seat and snapped open a leather briefcase; the way short tendrils of dark hair curled over the collar of his shirt as he bent his head in concentration. He hadn't once looked in her direction, Kylie remembered, at least not to her knowledge. And now that she faced the full attention of his dusky eyes, she knew for certain that he hadn't noticed her presence on the flight. She would have known, would have felt the touch of his gaze.

"I beg your pardon?" she asked, trying to disguise a flicker of uncertainty with a composed expression.

"Do you need some help with your luggage?" The chivalrous inflection threading his voice was oddly appealing.

"I've been hoping to catch the attention of a skycap, but there seems to be a noticeable lack of them." Looking at him with amusement, she said playfully, "I don't suppose you're—?"

His mouth completed the upward slant into a smile. "Just a former boy scout, I'm afraid. But I did earn a merit badge in luggage handling."

"Oh." A pleasurable ripple of discovery hesitantly dimpled her cheek. "And do you also assist little old ladies across the street?"

"But of course." Friendly amusement danced deep in his eyes. "I try never to discriminate on the basis of age, though, and you do look as if you could use some assistance."

She dropped a rueful glance at the awkward tangle of suitcases at her feet, knowing she probably appeared helpless, but unable to recover her usual aplomb. She met his eyes with a conceding grimace. "Yes, thank you. I'd appreciate your help. If you're sure you don't mind . . ."

He lifted a hand to still her doubts. "Say no more. My pleasure." A wayward strand of sable hair edged onto his forehead as he bent to look at her luggage.

An indefinable impulse to brush the dark hair into place tickled her fingertips and brought a stern mental reprimand. She wondered if it was possible to get jet lag on a ninety-minute flight from Denver.

His eyes skimmed from the luggage tags to her face with a cursory but inquiring glance at the ring finger of her left hand. "My pleasure," he repeated, "Miss Kylie Richards of San Diego."

There was a thin whisper of question in the words, and she found herself intrigued by his interest and the quiet charm of his husky voice. "You have the advantage, I'm afraid," she said with a questioning lift of her brows.

The charcoal-gray eyes frowned, then softened with understanding. "Nick Braden of San Francisco," he provided with a courtly nod.

"*Mister* Nick Braden?" Kylie couldn't resist stressing the unequal amount of information on marital status conveyed by their respective titles.

His lips formed a curve of droll appreciation. "*Mister* Braden, as in *Miss* Richards," he clarified. "But you can call me Nick. I sometimes forget to answer to Mister."

"All right, Nick. It's nice to meet you."

Her hand was suddenly tucked within his. A warm clasp, a brief touch that somehow made her feel utterly and completely feminine.

"And it's very nice to meet you—Kylie." He spoke her name as if savoring a newly discovered taste, and she liked the sound of it.

She liked the way he smiled, too, and the curious hint of a cleft in his chin. She liked the quiescent laughter hiding in his eyes. As he moved to lift her suitcases she noted the smooth play of muscles beneath his shirt and the understated power of his lean, sinewy legs. A tinge of color warmed her cheeks as she realized the direction of her appreciation. With a blink of surprise she looked away. Jet lag or no, there was no excuse for such a response to a man's simple courtesy.

When he straightened, a suitcase under his arm and one in each hand, she'd toned her bemused smile to a casually interested curve.

"Where to?" Nick asked.

Realizing that she didn't have the faintest idea what to tell him, Kylie caught herself from a betraying stammer and abruptly made a decision. "A taxi."

Slowly Nick returned the suitcases to the floor. "Is this your first trip to Santa Fe?"

"Well, yes, but—"

He nodded as if that explained everything, pursed his lips, and eyed her with a thoughtful frown. "I might warn you that it's a toss-up as to whether morning or a taxi will appear first."

Frustration welled and slid from her throat on a sigh. It had been a long day, and the end wasn't anywhere in sight. There wasn't much she could do now, except wait and hope that Alex would eventually either show up to get her or answer his telephone, which she had already rung several times. With a shrug Kylie smiled halfheartedly at Nick. "In that case I guess I'll just have to wait. Thanks for your offer of assistance, anyway."

"There's no need for that, Kylie." His voice took on a tone of command. "I phoned ahead for a rental car, which, with any luck, will be waiting out front. I'll take you to your hotel or wherever you're staying. Are you visiting friends in the area?" he added almost as an afterthought.

She nodded absently, considering his offer, discarding it, then considering it again. She couldn't just accept—could she?

Apparently Nick thought she not only could but already had. "I'll just check about the car and put your

14

luggage in the trunk, and we'll be ready to go. Would you like to stop somewhere for dinner?"

The question sounded almost rhetorical, and Kylie had the impression that she was being swept along by his casual assumption of authority. She started to correct him, to tell him that she didn't accept invitations on such short acquaintance, but an unexpected impulse stayed her tongue. She was not really sure what she was searching for, as her gaze moved over his tall, lithe body and paused to examine more closely the ruggedly attractive face. An assortment of fine lines at the corners of his eyes and mouth expressed his character with pride, confidence, and good humor. Determination lay only partially hidden in the firm set of his chin, and Kylie sensed that Nick Braden would make a formidable adversary and an equally devastating ally. It was evident he was a man unused to opposition, either real or imagined.

"Kylie?" He broke through her hesitation with a hint of impatience.

She suppressed a sudden tickle of amusement. Apparently Nick Braden wasn't used to waiting for an answer either. "Did you just invite me to dinner?" she asked and wondered what Miss Manners would do in this situation.

"Dinner and a safe delivery to your destination," he confirmed in a voice both persuasive and self-assured. "I'd be happy to show you my driver's license and my diner's club card if you'd like." As if aware of her lingering hesitation, he lifted a hand in mock solemnity. "And, scout's honor, there will be no mention of a trip to see my etchings."

Despite her best intentions Kylie felt herself responding to his teasing and the odd, almost off-center smile that slanted his lips. Like the affectionate clasp of a handshake, she felt his gaze reassuring her, erasing her doubts with an ease born of experience.

15

"Thank you," she heard herself saying. "Dinner would be very nice."

"Great." He turned before she had a chance to reconsider and began to gather her luggage into his arms again. Kylie watched him with a procrastinating trace of uncertainty. Her usually cautious nature had obviously gotten lost in his you-can-trust-me gray eyes. His offer of dinner hadn't done any harm, either, she thought as her stomach growled in silent agreement.

He straightened and took a step toward the exit. Then he stopped and glanced back at her. "I'm going to see about that car. Wait here. I'll be right back."

"Nick?" Kylie called before he could leave. "I think I'll make a phone call while you're doing that."

"Fine. Actually I should check in with my cousin too. Why don't you make your call. I'll take care of finding the car, phone my cousin, then meet you back here in fifteen minutes."

"I'll do that, Nick." She tried to hide the humor that laced her words. She badly wanted to challenge his take-charge manner just for the fun of seeing his amazement. She would have wagered all the money in her purse that few people, if any, even thought to question Nick Braden's authority.

"Fifteen minutes, then." His gaze held hers, and Kylie felt as if he were searching past the soft coffee-brown color of her eyes, looking for the spark of mischievous rebellion he must have heard in her voice. "Don't forget, Kylie."

"No." For the life of her she couldn't say another word, and with an effort she freed herself from his probing look. Decisively she turned and made her way toward the nearest phone, but halfway across the room she glanced over her shoulder. Nick was striding confidently through the doorway, her luggage firmly in hand.

Well, she was committed now, Kylie thought. Nick had

16

taken command of her evening, as well as her possessions, with unbelievable efficiency. And she wasn't even sure that she minded. It wasn't often she met a man who attracted and intrigued her as Nick Braden did.

Refusing to pursue that line of thought, Kylie walked to the telephone. She dug through the contents of her purse and again located the business card imprinted with the name Southwest Textiles, Inc., Santa Fe, New Mexico. Dialing the number penciled on the back of the card, she reminded herself that she was here to conduct a training seminar. If she wanted to prove the value of her ideas in a company as large and well respected as Southwest Textiles, then she'd have to concentrate on the business at hand, not on the appealing charm of dusky-gray eyes and a lopsided smile.

The ringing of the phone echoed hollowly in her ear, and she was just about to replace the receiver when she heard an answering click. "Yes?" The brusque, no-nonsense male voice replaced the mental image of Nick's dark good looks with a picture of Alex Jamison's sun-bleached hair, near-perfect profile, and deceptively innocent blue eyes.

"Alex? This is Kylie Richards."

"Kylie! What a surprise!" His tone changed almost magically to one of suave pleasure. "I didn't expect to hear from you until tomorrow. You haven't had a change in plans, have you?"

Kylie frowned, wondering if Alex typically forgot important commitments. "I haven't changed my plans, Alex, but I was beginning to wonder if you had. You did send the airline tickets, and I followed your instructions to the letter, but—"

"Lord, I didn't get the days mixed up, did I?" Alex interrupted with a groan. "Was I supposed to meet you at the airport today?"

"I assumed that someone would, but—"

"I'm sorry, Kylie," he pleaded. "I've been gone all day. Just walked in the door, in fact, and I didn't think about—" There was a pause, and Kylie thought she heard a distinctively feminine voice in the background. "Uh, Kylie?" Alex continued. "It's going to be a while before I can get there to pick you up. But now that I think about it, you might be able to catch a lift with—"

"I don't need a ride now, Alex. I—" She stopped herself from explaining the circumstances of her meeting with Nick and began again. "There won't be any problem getting into town. If you'd just give me the address of where I'm to stay, you won't have to worry about me at all." Not much chance of that either way, she thought wryly, since Alex didn't appear at all concerned about her welfare.

"Oh, that's great," he said with obvious relief. "I am sort of busy at the moment."

Kylie smothered an exasperated sigh, knowing it was useless to be upset with him. If she remembered correctly, Alex liked petite blondes with adoring eyes, simple tastes, and an intellect to match. "I'm sure your *job* keeps you very busy," she said with mock sympathy.

He had the grace to give an embarrassed laugh. "Well, you know how it is, Kylie."

"Yes, I do." She had no difficulty in remembering how busy he'd been when she'd met him at a business convention last spring; she'd competed with a succession of curvaceous blondes for his attention. Before she'd finally secured the contract, Kylie had begun to wonder if it was true that blondes did have more fun. "Why don't you tell me the address?" she prodded.

As Alex gave directions to the company housing where she was to stay, Kylie jotted the information in tiny print beneath his phone number on the business card. "The key will be under the planter of the big potted palm on the porch. You can't miss it. If you have any problems, call me. But you should find everything you need in the house. We keep it ready for visitors because the head office is always sending someone to check on things and stir up trouble for me." He released an aggrieved sigh into the phone. "You'd think that since the company is a family-run business, they'd trust me, but—"

Again Kylie heard the feminine voice in the background.

"Well, I'll be in touch with you later." Alex now sounded pressured and in a hurry to conclude the conversation. "Remember to call if there's anything you need."

"All right," Kylie began, then stopped when she heard the buzzing in her ear and realized she was talking to empty air. Shaking her head, she slipped the card into her purse and walked toward the airport entrance, where she was to meet Nick.

Kylie decided that under the circumstances it was lucky she'd accepted his offer of a ride. Otherwise she would have had to wait indefinitely at the airport. And even if a taxi hadn't proved so elusive, the cost would have put an extra strain on her already tight budget.

She drew in her breath sharply at the thought. Was she becoming so mercenary that she had to look at everything in terms of cost or savings? Kylie reprimanded herself for the negative attitude. A struggling new business was expensive, to be sure, but she wasn't destitute, not yet, anyway. And with the opportunity at Southwest Textiles there was no reason to think she wouldn't be successful.

Think positive, act positive, be positive. The words from the training manual came readily to mind, and she wondered if Nick Braden had ever taken an assertiveness course. Her lips formed a wry curve at the ridiculous idea. The confidence inherent in his every action was evidence that he'd been born with the quality. He'd never had to learn to be self-assured as she had.

Kylie sank into a chair in the lobby where she could see the entrance. In less than a minute she caught sight of Nick's tall, lean form across the room. A faint whisper of excitement stole through her as she saw him surveying the room. He was looking for *her,* and the knowledge made her heartbeat quicken with anticipation. It had been a long time since she'd felt such an instant attraction to a man, and she was suddenly very glad she'd agreed to have dinner with him. Even had she been able to afford a chauffeured limousine for the trip into town, Kylie knew she'd still be right where she was—waiting for Nick to see her and come to her side. She stood and lifted her hand to catch his attention.

Nick saw Kylie just as she rose and waved to him. He slid an appreciative glance over the graceful line of her throat and shoulders to the tantalizing silhouette revealed by the clinging fabric of her dress. Then with lingering enjoyment he observed the way the rich, chestnut hair framed her face with soft curls and her brows arched in a natural line above dark eyes screened by gold-tipped lashes. He watched her smile and liked the elusive dimple that flirted with the creamy perfection of her cheek. Again his eyes returned to the sensual curve of her breasts, and he felt his body tighten in response.

She looked different now from the forlorn slip of femininity that had first caught his attention. There was an air of distinction, of confidence, about her that intrigued him, a poised tilt to her head that belied his initial impression of uncertainty. She appeared at ease and in control now. A woman capable of handling herself—and any unwary man, Nick cautioned himself as he moved toward her.

"Hi." Kylie smiled a welcome.

"Ready?" he asked, reciprocating her smile as they turned together and walked to the exit. "Were you able to get in touch with your friends?"

She considered explaining that Alex was merely a business associate, then decided against it. "Yes," she answered simply. "Did you phone your cousin?"

Nick pushed open the door and let her precede him outside. "The line was busy, but it doesn't matter. I'll see him tomorrow."

Kylie tried to match her steps to his lengthy strides. She was breathless when he stopped beside a late-model car and held the door for her. "Thank you," she murmured as she slid onto the front seat. As he closed the door and walked around the front of the car, Kylie decided she'd never before met a man who evoked such an immediate physical response within her. She had a sudden feeling that her breathiness wasn't caused by the brisk walk to the car.

"We're all set." Nick slid behind the steering wheel and started the engine.

"Thanks for taking care of my luggage." She hoped her voice sounded stronger to him than it did to her. The closeness of his muscular body and the faint scent of his cologne weren't helping her to recover her breath. "And thanks for the ride into town too," she continued, determined to act as if that whispery vibration were her usual tone of voice.

His smile was easy, understanding, sincere. "My pleasure."

What might have been a trite rejoinder from someone else was a simple, believable statement from Nick. *My pleasure.* How had he made such a meaningless phrase convey so much?

My God, Kylie! She snapped her gaze to the front of the car. *Next you'll be hearing music when he speaks,* she scolded herself. Forcing the ridiculous tilt of her lips to a more sober angle, she resolutely stared out the window and managed to control the impulse to laugh when Nick clicked on the radio.

A soft symphonic melody drifted around her and brought her attention back to him. How wonderful that they had the same taste in music. "You must be a native," she said. "Or a frequent visitor."

Curiosity hovered on the arch of one dark brow. "Both, actually. I was born and raised here, and I'm often here on business." His smile was teasing. "But how did you know?"

"Elementary deduction, Dr. Watson." She made a grand gesture toward the dash. "Rental car, classical music. Not too many people could find that radio station on the dial unless they were familiar with the area."

"How do you know it wasn't already tuned to that station, Sherlock?"

Kylie met his eyes. "Was it?" she asked.

"No."

"That's what I thought. To be honest, though, I already had an idea you were a regular traveler to Santa Fe. On the plane this evening I thought—"

"Were you on the commuter flight from Denver? With me?" His incredulity was unmistakable. "That's impossible."

She couldn't help laughing then. "Impossible maybe, but true."

Nick shook his head disbelievingly as he braked the car, then made a smooth left turn. "I've definitely been working too hard. And to think if I had arrived earlier for that flight, I could have sat with you, and I would have had more time to get to know you."

It would take a strong woman to resist that line, Kylie thought, excusing the rapid flutter of her pulse. A much stronger woman than the marshmallow his persuasive charm was turning her into.

Groping for a safe topic of conversation, she focused her gaze on the last colorful rays of the sunset sky. "Beautiful sunset," she commented, trying not to be too obvious. "I've heard there's nothing lovelier than a New Mexico sky at sunset." It was all she could do to keep from making a face. Couldn't she have thought of something more original to say? "Really, lovely colors." Worse, she thought in disgust. Especially since the lovely colors were almost a memory in the already darkening twilight.

"Personally I prefer sunrise. But most of the artists I know disagree with me." Nick guided the topic of conversation from maudlin to interesting with enviable skill. "Of course, I've found that artistic temperaments thrive on disagreement anyway, so I try not to take their opinion to heart. Especially at this time of year, when the summer arts festival is in full swing." He shot her a cautious look. "You're not an artist, are you?"

"Strictly paint-by-number."

He nodded in seeming satisfaction. "I knew we were kindred spirits. My only excursion into the realm of painting hangs in awful splendor in my mother's bedroom."

"Appropriately titled *Santa Fe Sunrise*, no doubt."

He lifted his shoulders in a disarming shrug. "Well, there's no accounting for taste, you know. Which brings us to the restaurant and dinner. Do you like Mexican food?"

"Of course," Kylie answered, giving in to the delighted smile that tugged at her lips.

"Good." Nick manuevered the car into a parking space and turned off the ignition. "Usually I'd phone ahead for reservations, but there wasn't time tonight. We'll just hope there's a vacant table."

His voice was full of confidence, and Kylie thought

again that he wasn't used to any sort of opposition. Something about Nick Braden fairly shouted "success" to the world, and somehow Kylie knew that once they were inside the restaurant, there *would* be a vacant table.

Her intuition was right on target, she observed some twenty minutes later as she followed the beaming maître d' from the bar. She'd barely had time to sip the margarita Nick had ordered for her before they were being seated at a table in the dining area of the restaurant. Bright splashes of color along with the traditional Spanish decor of the Southwest lent an air of festivity to the room. Spicy scents mingled with the soft strum of a guitar.

"This is what I call atmosphere with a capital *A*." Kylie studied her surroundings with interest before she met the friendly warmth of Nick's gray eyes. "It reminds me of Old Town in San Diego. Have you ever been there?"

"My trips to southern California have always ended in Los Angeles." Nick leaned forward. "But if I'd had any idea that you were only a few miles away, every trip would have taken me to San Diego."

"Business trips?" Kylie asked, bypassing any verbal response to the compliment. "You must do a lot of traveling in your job."

"Not that much. Most of the time I stay close to the home office, though when there's any problem at the plants themselves, I'm always chosen as the troubleshooter."

Kylie widened her eyes in mock dismay at the term, and Nick laughed. "It isn't quite as ominous a title as it sounds. The problems usually are solved by reassuring the employees that they're adequately paid, insured, and safety-checked. Occasionally I have to investigate a new idea that the plant manager feels would increase production."

Her business sense jumped to eager attention at the words. "Is that why you're here?"

"Mmm-hmm." Nick lifted his glass and sipped his drink. His gaze rested lightly yet intimately on her lips, and Kylie felt her breath rise from her lungs to drift uncertainly in her throat. Willing herself to concentrate on what he'd said, she touched her finger to the salty rim of her glass.

"I like to see corporations that aren't afraid of innovative ideas. Too often high-level executives are paranoid about any new method that might upset the status quo and force some much-needed change." Noting his interested expression, Kylie warmed to her subject with enthusiasm. "In fact, I hope that in the near future companies will replace those aging, autocratic idiots who take up office space and oppose every fresh, new theory in favor of musty, outdated procedures. It's about time that the average employee can suggest—" She broke off her impassioned speech as she caught a glimpse of laughter in his eyes.

"Would you like me to order a soapbox for you?" he asked with a teasing grin.

"No, thanks." She couldn't suppress a reluctant smile. "I seem to have managed all right without one. Sorry, Nick. I'm usually not quite so vocal about my opinions."

"Don't apologize. Everyone should have a cause they feel strongly about."

"It's not that, exactly. I've been doing some promotional work for my business, and I keep running into brick walls when it comes to getting someone to listen. It's very frustrating when you don't even get the chance to present your ideas. But that's all about to change. I'm—" She stopped as the waiter arrived beside their table.

After an inquiring glance at her Nick took charge of ordering, and Kylie regarded him in thoughtful silence. It would be challenging to work with a man as assertive as Nick. Challenging, demanding, instructive, and satisfying.

Satisfying. Her mind lingered on the thought as she envisioned the two of them sitting side by side before a cozy fire discussing her ideas for a seminar. Nick would listen, would be interested in and accepting of new ideas. She would be able to tell him about— Common sense interrupted her daydream with indisputable logic. If she was sitting beside Nick after a draining day of training sessions, she wouldn't want to discuss business. She'd want to relax in his arms and feel—

With a start of surprise she realized he was speaking to her. "What?"

"I just asked if you wanted another drink." Amusement sparkled in his eyes.

"No, thank you. This is fine." Kylie wrapped her fingers around the slender stem of her glass and raised it to her lips. She touched the crystals of salt with her tongue before she sipped the drink. She was tempted to ask Nick if his company might be interested in hiring hers, but she didn't want to seem pushy. Again she ran her tongue along the frosted edge of her glass, then looked up, only to get lost in his eyes. Her breathing fluttered in that unexpected odd-even pattern that so exactly matched the sudden rapid beat of her heart. As if he couldn't help himself, Nick lowered his gaze to her mouth and traced the contours that badly wanted to tremble. Slowly she set her glass on the table and gave in to the purely visual touch that swept through her like a streak of lightning in a stormy sky. Sensuous, probing, and oddly unsettling, it left her feeling dissatisfied and somehow restlessly expectant. Kylie came to the belated realization that she should at least stammer a protest. But what could you say to a man who'd just, so tenderly, kissed you with his eyes?

"How long are you planning to stay in town, Kylie?"

From somewhere she managed to recover her voice. "I—uh—I'll be here about six weeks. What about you?"

"I think that might depend on you." The words caressed her with their huskiness. "And whether or not your friends will share your time with me."

"Oh." For a minute she couldn't seem to manage more than the breathless whisper. "Well, actually I'm not visiting friends."

His eyes were gray clouds of seduction as he reached across the table to cover her hand with his. "Good. Then I won't have to share you with anyone."

The pulse at the base of her throat skipped in confusion, and Kylie swallowed. It was definitely time she took command of the situation. Attractive as he might be, she'd only just met him. Summoning her poise, she smiled. "I'm on a business trip too."

He seemed to take the hint concealed in her crisp tones and withdrew his hand from hers. "I'd like to see you again, Kylie. Will you have dinner with me tomorrow night?"

She laughed softly. "We haven't even had dinner tonight."

"All right, then. Make it lunch tomorrow."

Pleasurable excitement bubbled inside her, but she tried to look suitably casual. "I think I'd better accept before you begin offering breakfast in—" *Bed.* The thought hovered in the air as if she'd spoken it aloud, and Kylie wanted to slide under the table.

With a gentlemanly arch of his brows Nick acted as if he didn't know what she had so obviously almost said. "If you'd like, we can meet for breakfast," he suggested.

"No." Kylie refused with an emphatic shake of her head. "Dinner tomorrow night will be fine." Mercifully the waiter arrived with their food, and she breathed a shaky sigh of relief. With studied calm she dipped a tortilla chip in the hot sauce and bit into it, hoping she would burn her tongue and thus prevent any further indiscretions.

By the time she'd dulled the edge of her hunger with the spicy *burrito*, her poise had returned.

"This is very good," she commented.

He nodded. "Would you like to meet me here tomorrow, or shall I come for you?"

Kylie almost gave him the address but then remembered that she had no idea of the next day's agenda. "I'll have to let you know, Nick. I'm not sure of my schedule yet. Is there some way I can get in touch with you in the morning?"

Nick curled his index finger through the handle of his coffee mug and lifted it halfway to his lips. "I'll be at the plant all morning. You can reach me there. The number's in the book, or you can dial information and ask for Southwest Textiles."

"Southwest Textiles?" Kylie repeated. "But that's where I'll be working."

The coffee cup clattered against the saucer, and alarm tingled the back of her neck as she registered the look of stunned surprise on his face.

"*You're* Management Movers?" he asked in a hoarse voice.

"Motivation Management," she corrected automatically. "That's the name of my company. We conduct management development seminars for businesses. Well, really, there's only me at the moment, but I'm planning to hire an assistant soon. Southwest Textiles is the first large firm to see the benefit of this type of training, and there's—" Self-consciously she stopped herself. "But you already know all about that, don't you? You probably were instrumental in authorizing the contract."

Nick avoided meeting her eyes as he took a long swallow of his drink. "No, Alex Jamison gets full credit for that."

"Oh, Alex." Kylie kept her tone bright and innocent, hoping against hope that she was misreading Nick's reaction. "I guess, then, he's the cousin you were calling at the airport."

"Yes, he gets full credit for that too."

Her spirits plunged at the portentous tone of his voice, but still she managed a careless smile. "It's a small world, isn't it?" At his skeptical expression her smile faltered, but she made herself continue. "Who would ever have thought we'd meet in such an unusual way? I'm here to direct a conference for your company, and you're here to—"

"Kylie," Nick interrupted, pinning her with a regretful but steady gaze, "I'm here to fire you."

Her heart plummeted and her mind raced in several directions at once. Shock and anger pushed a defensive response to her tongue, but Kylie made herself stop and think. She mustn't let him intimidate her. "You can't do that," she said finally and prided herself that she sounded as cool and authoritative as he had.

"I believe I just did." The sympathy in his eyes faded noticeably. "I'm sorry it turned out to be you, but that's the way it is."

That's the way it is. His words fell into the whirling chaos of her mind and restored order. Just like that. No questions. No explanations. Just, *That's the way it is.* Outrage inflamed her cheeks with hot color, but Kylie calmly lifted her napkin to her lips and returned it to her lap before she slanted a strained but composed smile toward Nick. The need to challenge his assumption of unimpeachable authority was no longer a mischievous impulse. This time she had too much at stake.

"I don't believe you understand the terms of the contract, Mr. Braden. My attorney was very thorough. A

cancellation requires advance notice—a *month's* notice."
She paused as his mouth firmed into a disapproving line.
Masking her inner trepidation, she matched his hard stare.
"In the long run, you know, a six-week seminar will be
much less expensive than a two- or three-year lawsuit."

His gaze didn't waver in the deliberate one-on-one confrontation, and as the tense, silent seconds crept past,
Kylie found it increasingly hard not to look away. Hidden
from his view, her fingers pleated the linen napkin in folds
of doubt.

"Is that the type of training you propose to give my
employees, Kylie?" His voice, low and intense, rippled
over her. "Do you teach them to assert themselves by
threatening legal action against the management? Tell me,
after the seminar do you stick around to oversee the mutiny, or do you scurry home to safety?"

The unjustness of his accusation refueled her temper.
"I've never led a mutiny. Of course, I've never before
worked with such an overbearing—"

"Autocratic idiot?" Nick supplied smoothly. "I believe
that was your term for anyone who didn't agree with your
line of reasoning."

"No. That's my term for anyone who doesn't take the
time to find out what he's talking about before he passes
judgment."

"And that's the way you see my decision to nullify your
contract?"

"How astute you are," she said through tight lips. "But
I should have known you would be. After all, there must
be *some* quality that got you into a plush office where you
can make arbitrary decisions instead of *working* for a living." Kylie knew she was burning bridges she couldn't
afford to rebuild, but she couldn't sit passively and allow
him to deprive her of this chance to prove herself. She
believed in the principles she taught, and if Nick would

only give her a fair hearing she could convince him of the value of the training sessions too.

The flash of anger in his eyes was quickly brought under control. "Look, Kylie. I'm sorry. I know you must be disappointed, but I'm sure you can understand my position."

"Certainly." Her voice shook with cool hauteur. "Just as, I'm sure, you can understand mine." With shaking fingers Kylie folded her napkin and placed it beside her plate. She pulled the strap of her purse over her shoulder. "Thank you for dinner."

Nick's hand closed around her wrist before she could get more than halfway out of her chair. "Sit," he commanded gruffly. "We may as well get this thing straightened out now." When she tilted her chin defiantly, his grip tightened. "I'm not going to let you walk out of here alone. The town is bulging at the seams with tourists and participants in the arts festival. It's no place to be on your own. Now sit down, and let's discuss this like two rational business people."

"Which one of us is not," Kylie said grimly. "Are you, Mr. Braden?"

"Sit," he repeated with the barest hint of a threat.

She sank to the edge of the chair and glared at him, wishing she could freeze the overconfident expression on his face. And to think she'd really liked him! God! She'd almost fallen all over herself liking him! "Let go of my arm," she snapped.

"And if I do?"

She leaned forward, her lips feigning a smile. "Now, what do you think?"

"I think you take this assertiveness training too seriously." His fingers loosened their hold, but his hand remained over hers.

31

"And you don't take it seriously enough. Offering your employees the opportunity to feel better about themselves and the job they do can be extremely beneficial to your company. The concept is new, but it works. Within two months you'll see a significant increase in production."

"Oh, really?" His gray eyes proclaimed a cynical disbelief. "Would you sign that in blood?"

Kylie held back a useless retort and suppressed the flood of disappointment she felt at his words. "Still afraid of a mutiny?"

His hand moved to the stem of his glass, and he watched her appraisingly before answering. "At the moment it seems a distinct possibility."

"You know," she said, her voice deliberately provocative, "if you're that insecure in your job, perhaps you should take the assertiveness course." She rose and faced him squarely. "Excuse me. I think I should phone Alex and let him know there's a—slight problem."

"Why don't you do that, Kylie." Nick stood, too, an impatient challenge mirrored in his eyes. "And while you're at it, ask him if there's a 'slight problem' with your accomodations."

Kylie's knees threatened to melt beneath her, but she kept her expression under strict control. "That's already been taken care of," she announced, quelling a rising uneasiness. "I'm staying in the company hou—" Her words ended in a horrified silence. "You mean, you're staying—?"

"Exactly."

Kylie drew a deep breath. "Well, then, all the more reason to call Alex now. He'll be able to straighten everything out."

Before Nick could command her to stay, she turned and walked toward the restaurant lobby. *Alex had better be able to straighten out the tangle,* she thought, her anger finding a new target. Although it didn't seem likely, he might not be aware of Nick's presence in town and the problem with the housing. But Alex must have known when he signed the contract that Cousin Nick wouldn't approve. Well, innocent or not, Alex was about to find out just how assertive she could be.

Kylie felt Nick's gaze follow her across the room, and inadvertently she remembered the gentle laughter in his eyes when he'd first touched her arm in the airport. She muttered an oath under her breath. A low, heartfelt "Damn."

Damn, Nick thought as he watched Kylie walk from the dining area. As he settled back in his chair and sipped at his now-watery margarita, he wished Alex were close enough to bear the brunt of his frustration. It was apparent that another test of executive power was in the offing—one of those battles that cast Alex in the innocent, just-trying-to-do-my-best-for-the-company role and Nick as the villain. If only Aunt Rosemary wasn't so insistent that her "little Alex" be the president of Southwest Textiles. And if only his grandfather hadn't laid the responsibility for seeing that nothing went wrong squarely on Nick's shoulders.

Frowning into his glass, Nick wondered if Alex had scheduled Kylie's flight to coincide with his own. It was exactly the sort of thing that delighted Alex. Setting up some sort of confrontation and then letting it take place while he, Alex, was safely away from any possible repercussions. It might be unfair, but Nick felt Alex could take full credit for this disastrous evening too.

Disastrous, he repeated silently as he visualized the furious sparkle in Kylie's dark eyes. For an evening that had begun with such promise, it had certainly deteriorated rapidly, and Nick wasn't even sure how it had happened. He could only remember that stubborn look on her face as she'd defied him.

Defied him! God, it was almost funny. Would be funny, if only she weren't so lovely. He drained the contents of his glass and muttered a low, heartfelt "Damn."

CHAPTER TWO

The office of Southwest Textiles was large and comfortable. Rays of early morning sunshine spilled through the window, providing the room with natural light. Woven rugs in vivid colors and designs adorned the rough-textured walls. Even in her present mood Kylie had to acknowledge the pleasant atmosphere of her surroundings.

As she settled into a chair her gaze slid over the burnished desktop to the cactus plant that occupied one corner. It wasn't the best example of desert flora, she admitted, but she felt a certain affinity with the thorny cactus. Spending a relatively sleepless night on the narrow sofa in Alex's apartment had been bad enough, but when she added the pouty hostility of his current live-in blonde . . .

Well, it was no wonder the morning had gotten off to a bad start. And to think she still had to face Nick Braden and somehow convince him to honor her contract. Fat chance of that happening, her mind jeered. Not after last night.

The memory of her retreat from the restaurant warmed

her cheeks with embarrassment. When she'd phoned Alex and asked him to come and get her, she'd told herself that she and Nick both needed some time to think things over.

But that wasn't true, she thought now. It had been cowardice to leave, pure and simple. Cowardice, too, to send Alex to pick up her luggage once she was safely entrenched in his apartment. And during the restless night she'd wished a dozen times that she'd stayed and brazened it out with Nick.

Kylie smoothed the polished cotton fabric of her skirt. She'd hoped the navy-blue sundress with its crisp, bolero jacket would make her look and feel professionally cool, but her confidence still hovered near ground level. The echo of Nick's voice telling her she was fired still thundered in her ears, and now—now she'd set herself up for another humiliating repeat.

The sound of tuneless whistling interrupted her dreary thoughts and directed them to the other occupant of the room. She tightened her lips and tapped one slim index finger against the other as she watched Alex fuss with the coffee maker. It was obvious he wasn't accustomed to the appliance, and Kylie had a feeling that on top of everything else he was about to ask *her* to make the coffee.

Irritation furrowed her brow as she decided to lay the blame for this whole awful situation at Alex's feet. The least he could have done was warn her there might be some opposition to the seminar, but when she'd pointed that out to him last night and again this morning, he'd told her not to give it another thought. "Leave everything to me," he'd said. "I'll take care of Nick."

Kylie would have liked to believe him, but common sense told her Alex was no match for his cousin. If Nick meant to rescind the contract, then she doubted that Alex could do a thing about it. If any persuasion took place, it was strictly up to her, and she didn't expect much support.

Alex straightened and cast a helpless glance at Kylie. "Do you think you might—?"

"No." The denial vented a tiny portion of her frustration but didn't really ease her tension.

A frown almost marred the perfection of his profile, but he caught himself and restored the amiable facade that grated on Kylie's nerves. If there was anything worse than knowing a disaster was imminent, she thought, it was having someone assure you there was absolutely nothing to worry about.

"Mr. Jamison?"

The door opened, and a young dark-haired woman stepped into the office. Her blue eyes met Kylie's brown ones with friendly inquiry but widened in alarm at the sound of Alex's voice.

"Bunny! Thank God! Where have you been?"

Rosy color flooded the woman's cheeks as she turned. "Oh, Mr. Jamison, I'm so sorry I'm late. There was an accident on the highway, and the traffic was backed up—"

"Never mind, Bunny. Just fix some coffee for us, would you? I can't seem to get it right. The first pot was thick enough to chew, and when I added water, it leaked all over everything." Alex lifted a soggy towel to illustrate his words, and Kylie thought he looked like a naughty child explaining a spill to his mother.

Bunny hurried to take the towel from his hands. "Mr. Jamison, I'm sorry. You shouldn't be doing that. Here, let me. I'll get this cleaned up and make fresh coffee at once."

Alex stepped back with a self-satisfied look that lowered him another notch in Kylie's estimation. As he walked to the desk she watched Bunny wipe the water from the table and floor.

"Your secretary?" she asked, expecting Alex to make an introduction.

"Yes. That's Bunny." He seated himself behind the

desk and clasped his hands on the desktop. "All right, Kylie. Why don't we get started with the preparations for this seminar?"

Surprised that he'd ignored the common courtesy of an introduction, Kylie lifted her brows and glanced pointedly at the other woman.

"She'll have the coffee ready in a few minutes," Alex said, misinterpreting the reason for Kylie's gesture. "Bunny's very efficient."

He bestowed the compliment in a cavalier tone of voice that made Kylie wish Bunny would efficiently pour the coffee over him. "Now, what should we tackle first?" he asked.

"I think you—" Kylie cut short the reprimand. With an inner shrug she ignored his rudeness and concentrated on her own problems. "First we need to discuss the housing arrangements and decide where I can live for the next few weeks."

"You're welcome to stay with me," he offered halfheartedly.

"You'd have a whole lot of explaining to do if I agreed to that, now, wouldn't you?" She refused with a shake of her head. "No, thanks, Alex. It's too crowded at your place."

He grinned. "I thought it was kind of cozy last night."

"Well, you're the only one who thought so," Kylie said dryly. "Your—uh—roommate didn't seem to take to the idea of sharing the apartment, even for one night."

"No, she didn't, did she?" He didn't seem bothered by that fact, Kylie noted as his eyes took on a pleased sparkle. "She tends to be possessive at times," he continued in a thoughtful tone. "And she was annoyed because I brought you home with me. I suppose if I expect a welcome this evening, I'd better make it up to her." He turned to his secretary. "Bunny, call the florist this morning and have something sent to my apartment for Miss Vandemere. A dozen—no, better make that two dozen red roses."

"Miss Vandemere prefers *pink.*" The hint of curtness in Bunny's voice was instantly disguised, but Kylie was sure she hadn't imagined it. "You always send her pink roses, Mr. Jamison."

"You're right, Bunny, as usual. Make it two dozen pink roses." He turned to Kylie with a chauvinistic wink that set her teeth on edge. "That takes care of placating my roommate for the moment. Now, what shall I do with you?"

She knew he was referring to the housing arrangements again, but she couldn't resist some feminine retaliation. "Personally," she said with wide-eyed innocence, "I prefer yellow roses."

Alex started to chuckle, then faltered into a fake cough as he watched her uncertainly. "Yellow?" he finally asked with a weak smile, making an obvious effort to regain his aplomb.

Kylie bit back a laugh and nodded. "That's so thoughtful of you, Alex. Thank you."

"Don't mention it. My pleasure. Uh—Bunny? Would you—?"

"I'll take care of it for you, Mr. Jamison." Bunny set a steaming mug on the desk before him and turned to Kylie. "Would you like some coffee, Miss—?"

"Richards," Kylie answered, sharing the amusement shining in Bunny's blue eyes. "But please call me Kylie. And you're . . . Bunny?"

"Stephanie," Bunny said almost hesitantly. "Stephanie Scott. Mr. Jamison is the only one who calls me Bunny." A blush crept into cheeks already rosy with color. "He hired me a few years ago just before Easter. You know . . . Easter—Bunny?"

Kylie managed to catch her jaw before it dropped. Her

gaze flew to Alex, who appeared to be absorbed in sipping his coffee, and then she looked again at his secretary. Stephanie's obvious embarrassment was the only thing that kept Kylie silent.

"It's nice to meet you, Stephanie." Kylie employed her best putting-people-at-ease voice and added an encouraging smile. "And I don't care for any coffee now, but when I do, I can pour it myself. Thank you, anyway."

Stephanie nodded and started toward the door. "Is there anything else, Mr. Jamison?"

"No." He paused, then called to her again. "Bunny? Nick's in town. You might keep that in mind."

A look of understanding passed between Alex and his secretary before she walked from the room and closed the door behind her.

Kylie arched her brows. "That sounds highly suspicious, Alex. You should be more careful. I might be a corporate spy."

"I almost wish you were." His tone was serious, not at all like the bantering reply she'd expected. "It would be poetic justice if there were something to hide. I'd love to see Nick's face—" Alex broke off with a shrug and leaned back in the chair. "There isn't anything suspicious about it. When my cousin pays a visit, Bunny runs interference for me and keeps him out of my hair."

"I thought you told me you could handle Nick."

"I can," he said with a fierce frown. "And I will. You can ignore Nick's threats and go ahead with your plans for the seminar. I hired you, and he's not going to veto my decision, even if I have to take this to the Board of Directors."

Kylie assumed an expression of mild interest, but anger uncoiled inside her. It was beginning to sound as if Alex were using her to seek some sort of corporate advancement over his cousin, and she didn't like the idea one bit.

40

The thought that she and her newborn company might be pawns in a game of executive politics tightened her fingers into fists. Well, whatever the reason for this tug-of-war, she refused to get caught in the middle. She was here to do a job, and she intended to do it. And when she was through, Alex Jamison and Nick Braden would feel the sting of her success.

She relaxed her fingers. "All right, Alex. I'm ready to begin this morning. First I want to do some basic background research on the area, so I'll need a car or some other means of transportation. It will probably take two or three days to gather the information I need, so we can schedule the first session for a week from today. I'll need one or two people to help during the actual sessions, and as soon as you can manage it, I need a list of employee names and a job description for each. And I mean a real job description, not just their working title."

"This is a little more involved that I thought," he said. "You should have told me to take notes."

"I shouldn't have to tell you things like that, Alex. As an executive, you owe it to yourself and the company you work for to use your time efficiently. Trusting your memory almost always means repetition, and repetition wastes time. With a minimum amount of effort you can train yourself to take concise notes that will make your time work effectively for you."

"Sorry I mentioned it."

She smiled at his rueful expression. "You're going to get your money's worth from this seminar, Alex." *Whether you like it or not,* she added silently.

"That's reassuring," Nick commented from the doorway. "Considering how much this amusing little diversion is going to cost him."

Alex practically catapulted to his feet, and Kylie's heart

jerked in a startled duplication of his action as her gaze swung toward the doorway.

Nick filled the space, his shoulders leaving only a narrow margin on either side. He seemed taller than she remembered and even more attractive. His dark hair feathered away from his rugged features, and his gray eyes scanned the room with lazy interest. In a light-blue suit with a pinstripe shirt and dark tie, he looked powerfully male—devastatingly male—and Kylie felt her skin tingle with sheer physical awareness of him.

"Good morning, Kylie. Alex." Nick advanced into the room with an air of command. Alex straightened his tie, adjusted the lapels of his tan western-style sports coat, and stepped from behind the desk, allowing Nick to take the position of authority.

Kylie watched this silent power play with a blend of resentment and comprehension. It was impossible not to resent Nick's confident, take-charge manner, but his action was understandable. Nick had only done what Alex clearly expected him to do.

Making a mental note to give Alex top priority on her training list, Kylie kept her gaze focused on Nick.

He sat in the chair Alex had vacated and lifted a typed report from the corner of the desk. Apparently ignoring everything and everyone around him, Nick began to shuffle through the pages. Kylie felt herself bristling, even though she felt sure he had no conscious intention of patronizing either Alex or herself. But conscious or not, it was a manuever that accomplished exactly that, and she recognized it. Nick was in command, and she would have to wait on his convenience. Well, that sort of thing might intimidate Alex, but it wouldn't work with her, and Nick might as well discover the fact right now.

Sitting straighter, Kylie released a throaty ripple of laughter, calculated to catch him off guard. When he looked up, she met his eyes with reckless daring. "You look rested, Nick. It must be wonderful to enjoy the sleep of the innocent when you have so much on your conscience."

He made no answer, but the faint tightening of his lips assured her of his attention. She hesitated for a fraction of a second, sensing rather than seeing Alex's warning glare. Then, with an inner shrug she decided it was time Alex showed some backbone.

"After all," she continued, speaking to Nick in a mildly accusing tone, "it can't be every day that you ruin a perfectly good dinner by attempting to fire your dinner companion from her job and then appropriating her bed for your own use. That's almost unforgivable."

"I was willing to share, but you chose Alex's accommodations instead, so don't blame me if you had to sleep on the sofa." There was a note of challenge in Nick's voice. "And while we're on the subject I think it's almost unforgivable that you walked out on me last night. You might at least have let me know you were leaving with Alex."

"I knew that with your perception you'd figure it out for yourself. I hated to embarrass you by sending a Dear John note with the waiter."

His eyes flashed with steely amusement beneath the dark threat of his brows. "You're right. It's much less embarrassing to stare for more than half an hour at an empty chair."

Kylie lifted her shoulders in a sympathetic shrug. "Life is lonely at the top, you know."

For an infinitesimal tick of the clock, his gaze held her, silently weighing her courage and daring her to push him too far. Then he shook his head, muttered something under his breath, and resumed his study of the papers in his hand, putting her right back in the position where she had started.

"I'm sorry," she said blandly. "I couldn't hear what you said. Was it anything important?"

All the amusement had vanished from his gray eyes when he looked up. "I said, *damn.* You know, Kylie, it's not surprising that you've never worked with a large corporation before if you're always so impertinent to your prospective employers."

Irritation replaced the bantering tone of her earlier remarks. "But you're not my employer, Nick. Not even my prospective employer. I have a contract signed by the president of Southwest Textiles, and I'm answerable to him and only to him. Isn't that right, Alex?" Without compunction Kylie threw the question at Alex and waited for him to sink or swim.

"She's right, Nick. I hired her to teach a crash course in management skills, and she's not leaving until it's done." Alex's voice expressed more determination than Kylie had believed possible, but she cringed inwardly at his description of her seminar.

Nick stared at his cousin in pensive surprise, and then he pushed back the sleeve of his coat and glanced at his watch. "Let's see," he said, shifting his gaze to Kylie. "I've got about five minutes free this morning. That ought to give you enough time to teach me how to develop management skills."

Kylie didn't even blink at his gibe. "Sorry, Nick. I prefer to teach someone who has real potential."

He leaned forward across the desk, his hands clasped and a tiny cleft of irritation etched in his firm chin. Kylie braced herself by curving her fingers inconspicuously around the arms of her chair.

"Miss Richards," Nick began, his voice deliberate and cool, "contract or no contract, you're—"

Alex intervened by clearing his throat and stationing

himself behind Kylie. "Now look, Nick. This was my decision, and you'll just have to—"

The buzz of the intercom cut into the room, and Alex, with a frustrated sigh that didn't quite match his relieved expression, moved to the phone. "Yes, Bunny? Yes—all right. Tell him I'll be there as soon as I can." He replaced the receiver and looked apologetically at Kylie. "Sorry, but there's a problem at the warehouse. I'm afraid I'll be gone all morning. You'll have to work out the seminar arrangements with Nick." Alex directed a firm stare toward his cousin. "And I expect it to be done without any further complications."

As Kylie watched him stride confidently from the room she had to control a curious impulse to giggle. She'd underestimated Alex. Apparently he could be very assertive—when on the retreat.

"Pretty slick arrangement, don't you think?" the hint of anger in Nick's voice had given way to trenchant humor.

"Arrangement?" Kylie turned to meet his eyes. "You mean the way he dumped you in my lap?" She smiled sweetly. "In a matter of speaking, of course."

"Of course," Nick agreed dryly as he relaxed in his chair. "It just always amazes me that some crisis seems to arise within ten minutes of the time I enter this office."

"That ought to tell you something."

"It tells me that Alex hired a damn good secretary."

"If that's true, then I'm surprised you haven't tried to fire her." Kylie crossed her legs and felt a ripple of feminine vanity when she noticed Nick's attention wander in that direction.

"I'm not quite the tyrant you seem to think I am, Kylie. I don't veto every decision Alex makes, regardless of what he's told you. Besides, this office needs Stephanie. Sometimes I think she's the only competent employee we have here."

"Then maybe you should make her the president of Southwest Textiles," Kylie said, wondering if she could provoke that tiny cleft in his chin into making a reappearance. "Or are you too chauvinistic to consider a woman for an important executive position?"

Nick's jaw tightened with impatience, then relaxed. "Are you always this much trouble to work with?"

"To work with? No." Kylie shook her head and smiled a slow, soft smile. She pushed from her chair, walked to the window, and running her fingers through her chestnut curls, stared at the textile mill that sprawled before her. "How many employees do you have here?" she asked, just to show him she was capable of politeness. "Alex estimated the number at somewhere between four and five hundred."

"Six hundred thirty-two, including the office personnel. The type of seminar you propose could produce a sizable mutiny. Maybe you can understand my caution if I tell you that Southwest Textiles isn't famous for its labor-management relationship. There's been trouble in the past, and I can't take the risk of stirring up any more."

Kylie turned with an exasperated sigh. "The training I offer will reduce that risk, not increase it. Why is it so hard for you to see that? If you open avenues of communication with the employees, they won't be so quick to blame the administration for everything that goes wrong. Give them some options, and this company will reap the benefits."

"That makes a great theory, Kylie, but not good business sense."

"It does, Nick. Give me the opportunity, and I'll prove it."

He twisted a pencil back and forth in his hands as he watched her. "You don't make it easy to refuse."

"Then don't. I realize that, given the choice, you would never have hired me, but I'm here now, and I do have a contract. I believe in developing positive thinking skills and in training individuals to use those skills on the job."

"I don't doubt your sincerity, Kylie. I just don't think you can accomplish what you say you can."

"Surely you've read the recommendations in the promotional material I mailed to Alex."

Nick stilled the movement of the pencil and leaned forward. "Recommendations from two companies with a third the employees of Southwest and with no history of labor disputes."

"Nick," she began and then paused to quell the note of pleading in her voice. "I don't see any way this seminar could precipitate the kind of employee problems you're talking about. I'm certainly not going to promote dissension among the workers. When it comes down to it, I have much more at stake than you. If anything should go wrong during or after the training, my company and all I've invested in it won't be worth two cents."

"It's not the same sort of risk."

Kylie sighed, knowing she was losing the battle. "Progress always involves a certain amount of risk."

"Resorting to philosophical arguments, Kylie?"

"If I thought it would change your mind, I'd be happy to argue all day." She turned to the window again and stared sightlessly at the mill outside. "You know, Nick, I really am disappointed in you. I expected you to be more open to new ideas. Last night you seemed interested—"

"I was interested. I still am."

His voice, soft and vibrant behind her, caught her by surprise. Wondering how he could have moved to her side without a betraying sound, she turned and looked straight into his mysterious smoke-gray eyes.

"What?" She frowned and felt confusion shape a dimple in her cheek.

"I'm interested in you, Kylie."

As a woman, not as a professional. It was an insult neatly rolled inside a compliment, but, she thought, it was still an insult. And it annoyed her out of all proportion. "Oh, I see." Kylie hid her feelings behind a superficial smile. "Maybe I should approach this problem from a different angle. Would you prefer that I persuade you to honor my contract with a few feminine wiles, Nick?"

"Kylie," he said with quiet warning, "you know that isn't what I—"

"Wait," she crooned in dulcet tones, no longer bothering to conceal her irritation. "I might make you an offer you can't refuse. I would have changed tactics sooner, but I gave you credit for being more professional than Alex. Silly of me, wasn't it? If I'd known that all I had to do to get this job was stroke your ego and . . ."

The sentence trailed off suggestively as her fingers toyed with the lapels of his suit. In some distant corner of her mind she was shocked at her own audacity, but she couldn't seem to stop. Her hands pressed against his chest as she raised her lips to rest intimately against his mouth.

A searing response jolted through her at the touch, but Nick stood rigidly still. His heart pounded evenly against her palms as she caressed the outline of his lips with her tongue. She tasted him, teased him, but wasn't able to evoke a response from him. Hating and yet admiring his control, she finally stepped back and faced his cool stare.

"What's wrong, Nick? Or are you always this much trouble to—work with?"

His hands slid up her arms to grip her shoulders with biting impatience. "That little display of defiance was uncalled for, Kylie. But if you insist on finding out just how much trouble I can—"

A tap on the office door left the words hanging in midair, but it wasn't hard to interpret his meaning. Her irritation faded as quickly as it had come. Maybe she had jumped to the wrong conclusion.

"Miss Richards?"

Kylie heard the door open and recognized Stephanie's voice, but she couldn't seem to shift her gaze from Nick to the doorway.

"What is it, Stephanie?" Nick asked without looking around.

"Mr. Jamison wanted me to give these to Miss Richards."

Blinking at the unexpectedly crisp tone, Kylie managed to free herself from Nick's hold. She walked toward Stephanie, noting the militant sparkle in the secretary's blue eyes. The animosity seemed directed at Nick, though, because Stephanie smiled easily as she extended her hand to Kylie. "These are the keys to a company car which Mr. Jamison has arranged for you to use. There's also a key to the house, the *company* house." Her blue eyes flicked a brief challenge at Nick, then switched back to Kylie. "Mr. Jamison said he didn't expect any problems, but you could get in touch with him later if necessary."

Kylie closed her fist over the keys and, despite her best effort, looked to Nick for approval.

He studied her clenched hand with hooded appraisal before turning a charming smile on Stephanie. "Thank you. Has Alex called from the warehouse? Did he get things under control?"

"He hasn't phoned," she answered politely but with no hint of a reciprocal smile. "I'm certain that Mr. Jamison has handled the problem in his usual efficient way. There's no need to worry about it."

Expecting Nick to rise to the challenge with a quelling display of authority, Kylie watched in amazement as he simply nodded. Stephanie bit her lower lip, and then, with an odd little sigh, she left the room.

"Hmmm," Kylie murmured, glancing from the door to Nick's impassive face. "Offhand I'd say you rate pretty low on her list of favorite employers. Have you been trying to intimidate her too?"

Nick eyed Kylie with a frown, then moved to sit on the corner of the desk, one leg draped casually over the edge. "I don't try to intimidate anyone."

"I know. It comes naturally, doesn't it?"

His lips tightened, and Kylie watched his chin, hoping to see that fascinating indentation, but his skin remained smooth. "I made the mistake of getting angry with Alex once when Stephanie was present. She's never forgiven me for calling him an incompetent idiot. In case you haven't noticed, Stephanie thinks Alex Jamison is just this side of a damn miracle." Nick shook his head. "She's been hopelessly in love with him for years."

Kylie lifted her gaze from the intriguing movement of his mouth. "Why hopelessly?"

"She isn't a blonde."

"Oh, Nick," Kylie protested with a short laugh. "Surely that doesn't make a difference."

"Not to me, anyway." He folded his muscular arms across his chest and shrugged. "But my cousin's personal life doesn't matter. What he does with this mill makes a lot of difference, though."

"And that brings us right back to—"

"You," Nick supplied. "You and whether you go or stay."

"I didn't realize there was a choice." She caught her breath as a flicker of hope surfaced. "Does that mean you might consider—?"

Nick watched her and correctly interpreted the sudden sparkle in her dark eyes. There might be hell to pay later, but he knew he wasn't going to let her return to San Diego. Not just yet, anyway. "I seem to be outnumbered three to

50

one," he said. "With you, Alex, and Stephanie aligned against me, I feel pressured into giving you a chance."

Kylie didn't dare breathe in case she was imagining the whole thing. "Would you mind repeating what you just said?"

"You heard me. You can hold your seminar, but—"

"Thank you, Nick. This means so much—"

"Kylie," he interrupted in a firm voice, "there are some stipulations. First I want you to agree that if I tell you there's a problem—any problem at all—you'll stop the sessions at once."

"There won't be any prob—"

"Agreed?"

She nodded. "But there won't be—"

"Second," he said, ignoring her protest, "I can only let you have three weeks."

"The training requires six full weeks, Nick. You can't expect—"

"Three weeks. Take it or leave it."

"You don't understand, Nick. I have to research the area and the mill itself. That's important, and I can't do it and still have time for the sessions."

"I'll help you in the evenings. I can give you information about the jobs, and I'm familiar with Santa Fe, so that won't be a problem."

Kylie fastened her attention on his first sentence and narrowed her eyes thoughtfully. "I don't work in the evenings, Nick."

He arched a brow in deliberate dispute. "Working evenings is better than not working at all."

"If you think I'm going to—" she began hotly.

"I don't think anything of the sort. Try listening to what's said, Kylie, and keep these displays of outraged virtue to yourself. I haven't said one thing that merits your

51

annoyance. It's only your interpretation that makes the comment suggestive or not, as the case may be."

"Really? Well, that's not the way I see it. You—" Kylie clamped her mouth shut. What on earth was she doing? Nick had just given her the job, and she was quarreling with him. Much as she disliked the idea, an apology seemed to be in order.

"Let's finish the arrangements," he said. "What materials will you need and when?"

The apology slid down her throat, and with a resigned curve of her lips she answered, describing each item in detail. He took notes, of course. Neat, concise notes that annoyed her irrationally.

"Anything else?" he asked when she'd finished. "Subversive literature? An arsenal maybe? Are you sure you don't want me to order a pirate's patch for your disguise?"

She smiled at his attempt to lighten the mood. "That won't be necessary, Nick. But couldn't you stretch that three weeks to six?"

"Sorry. Three weeks is the most I can spend in Santa Fe right now, and I'm not about to leave you on your own." He snapped his fingers. "That reminds me. The woman who usually does the cooking and cleaning at the house is on vacation, so I'll take care of dinner tonight, but tomorrow it's your turn."

"My turn?" Kylie stiffened and swung an accusing gaze to meet his bland look. "I thought there wasn't going to be any problem with the housing arrangements."

"You mean you object to sharing the kitchen duty?"

"Perceptive, as usual, Nick. I object to sharing the kitchen or any other room in the house."

"All right. You can make dinner every night. I'm adaptable."

Her breath escaped in an angry rush. "That's not what I meant!"

"Then what did you mean, Kylie?" The way he shifted his weight from the desk and started toward her was as disquieting as the unamused tone of his voice. He stopped in front of her and grasped her wrist in one hand while taking a firm hold on her chin with the other.

Kylie lifted her arm and then let the key chain slip from her fingers. Against her conscious decree her palm came to rest on his chest.

"What did you mean?" he repeated. "There are three bedrooms in the house. I sleep in one, and you can take your pick of the other two. Now, if you meant that you object to sharing the house, then by all means, find yourself somewhere else to stay. I'm sure Alex could be persuaded to let you spend another night on his couch. Other than that, I think you'll find the town crowded at this time of year. But if you want to use part of your three weeks to find something, be my guest." His fingers tightened, tilting her chin up. "And if you meant you object to sharing my bed, then all I can say is you should wait to be asked."

Kylie drew in her breath. "You're not going to intimidate me, Nick Braden! If I decide to stay at the house, I won't put up with this kind of behavior. I'm giving you fair warning. I won't—"

His mouth smothered her defiance with a firm insistence that teased her rebellion into retreat. She wanted badly to respond to the tempting taste of his lips, but she told herself to remain passive. Just as he'd been when she'd tried to arouse him. Fighting the sweet intoxication of his kiss, she trembled and drew on all her inner resources just to remain still. A slow shiver started in her knees and crept inch by inch up her legs, and her heart pulsed. It was all she could do to stay upright and not allow her body to sway against his for support.

Whirling dizzily, disjointed thoughts raced through her

mind, and her lips ached. Kylie moved them cautiously and was appalled by the sensual longing that raged within her. After that first tentative movement she was no longer in control, and she returned his kiss with only a remnant of caution.

Sensing the change in her, Nick drew back and loosened his grip on her chin. His eyes were dark, but Kylie thought she saw a glimmer of triumph there, and she rallied her sagging defenses.

"I won't cook for you either," she whispered.

"Damn, Kylie. Don't you ever shut up?" He captured her lips once more with tender and sensitive possession. And this time she didn't even try to tell her body to resist. Her heart just wasn't in it. She curved her arms around his neck and let her good intentions drain away.

When he raised his head, she felt limp, and it took a considerable effort to open her eyes. "Speechless?" he asked. "I should have tried this method sooner. It seems to have a debilitating effect on your vocal cords."

"Fortunately it's only temporary." Kylie knew she sounded weak and breathy, but she plunged on. "I'm going to need my voice when I start looking for a place to stay."

He smiled, and that intriguing cleft appeared in his chin. He slipped an arm around her shoulders and walked to the door. "Well, good luck. You'd better get started." He opened the door, then placed a detaining hand on her arm. "Wait."

She watched as he retraced his steps and bent to retrieve the key chain she'd dropped. When he returned to her, he dangled the keys over her outstretched palm. "Will I see you tonight?" he asked huskily.

"I don't know."

"You know, Kylie. You know damn well."

She let her lips form a noncommittal reply. "You say that too often."

His brows arched in a question. "What?"

"Damn," she answered. "You say it too often. It's a bad habit, you know. Especially for an executive."

He frowned as if he couldn't believe what she'd said. "I'll be d—" He broke off and grimaced. "Is this part of the training? Maybe I'd benefit from private lessons. What do you think?"

"I think it would be a waste of time. I was merely making an observation, not offering my services as a tutor."

"We can discuss it after dinner while you're doing the dishes."

She placed her hand on the doorknob. "Not a chance. You'll be eating alone." Unable to resist one last remark, she turned, then looked over her shoulder. "If you're not careful, Nick, dining alone could become a habit."

"I don't think so. At least not tonight."

"I won't be there."

He smiled. A slow devastatingly confident smile. "You'll be there, Kylie."

With a dismissing tilt of her chin Kylie swept through the doorway, wishing she could have the last word. But even as the door closed behind her and she faced Stephanie's curious eyes, Kylie knew there wasn't a thing she could have said.

She had a feeling that Nick was right. She would be at the company house this evening, probably full of excuses and rationalizations, but there nonetheless.

"Is something wrong?" Stephanie asked politely. "Mr. Jamison asked me to help you in any way I could."

"Thanks, Stephanie, but I'm afraid it's too late." With a casual wave Kylie hurried from the outer office, leaving the secretary looking bewildered.

First things first, Kylie decided as she stepped from the building into the hot summer sunshine. She'd look over the training manual and refresh her memory on the assertiveness principles. With Nick and the imminent prospect of facing refractory hotel clerks, it looked as if she was going to need every advantage that being assertive could give her.

CHAPTER THREE

Like a canvas awaiting the stroke of a brush, the sky stretched overhead, a canopy of indigo blue. Here and there the rosy haze of sunset made its final stand against the deepening twilight. One star and then another winked at Kylie, promising a finished portrait of night if only she would linger outside.

Drawing a deep breath of the cool air, Kylie tried to separate the interwoven scents of mountain juniper and the desert plants that decorated the patio. She knew it was an exercise in futility, but it was enjoyable just the same.

Closing her eyes, she lay perfectly still on the chaise longue and listened to the clatter of dishes in the kitchen behind her. Nick was making sure she heard each plate as he put it away in the cabinet.

Serves him right, she thought. It was bad enough that he'd halved the amount of time she needed for the seminar, but she had spent—no, wasted—an entire day because of him. Kylie frowned as she remembered the rejections she'd received from polite but firm hotel clerks. She wished she could take a fifteen-minute nap for every time she'd heard the arts festival mentioned. And each time she'd heard it, her irritation with Nick had increased.

By some process of distorted logic she had decided that if he hadn't told her she wouldn't find another place to stay, she wouldn't have been so determined to find one. She had driven in circles, walked for blocks, and discovered parts of Santa Fe that even the natives probably didn't know about. All to no avail. The only vacancies she had found were either extravagantly expensive or far from being suitable.

This company house was much more than suitable, she had to admit. It was spacious and quiet, and Kylie had been very glad to reach it at the end of a tiring and frustrating day. Despite the fact that Nick had seemed irritated by her late arrival, despite the fugitive tingle of pleasure she'd felt at seeing him again and quickly hidden behind a veil of defensiveness, Kylie thought she'd never been so glad to have a roof over her head.

And what a roof. This smaller version of a hacienda offered luxuries that no hotel could afford. The U-shaped house bordered the patio garden where she now relaxed. Inside, a tiled entryway opened onto a spacious room that contained both living and dining areas. The only bedroom she had entered, her bedroom by virtue of the luggage that Nick had placed there, was a peaches-and-cream delight with every possible comfort. The adjoining bath contained a huge sunken tub and a separate shower enclosed by crystal-clear glass panels. Done in black and silver, it was easily the most sinful-looking room she'd ever seen. She was looking forward to a steamy, hot, and very luxurious bath before bedtime.

Yawning at the enticing thought, Kylie stretched lazily on the chaise and admitted that this house also held an added attraction for her. To her chagrin she couldn't deny that Nick was definitely an attraction. And a potential hazard, she thought as another plate clattered loudly in the stillness.

He was so sure of himself and of her. He hadn't even looked surprised when she'd walked in the door earlier. "Your dinner's in the kitchen," he'd said, proving he'd never doubted her eventual arrival. "I'll get your luggage and put it in your room while you're pouring us both a glass of milk."

"I hate milk," she had answered, asserting her objection to his autocratic manner. The minor declaration of independence had only won her a half-annoyed, half-amused look that fired her determination to challenge him at every possible opportunity.

But Nick had effectively stayed out of reach, via the telephone, while she had explored the house, changed her clothes, and finally eaten her dinner. He'd entered the kitchen just as she was draining the last drops of milk from her glass.

She had felt his silent laughter and perversely wanted to share in his amusement. As he drank from his glass Kylie had fidgeted with her silverware, conscious of the purely physical impact he had on her senses. And when he turned on the faucet to begin cleaning up, she'd escaped to the patio with an excuse about having an allergic reaction to the dishwashing liquid. She was actually far more concerned about her reaction to Nick, but she hoped that wasn't obvious to him.

Opening her eyes, she traced the outline of the Big Dipper and wondered how she would manage to live in the same house with him and still keep a sane distance between them.

A gentle breeze brought the fleeting memory of another night spent in the mountains. It seemed a century ago, but the night had been much like this one: soft scents, a star-filled sky, a man who made her heartbeat quicken.

Colin had made it sound so romantic, and the thought that he did not mean it to be a platonic night never once entered her mind. Of course, she'd been only sixteen and so incredibly naïve. Kylie shook her head, remembering Colin's frustration when she wouldn't stop crying. He'd paced the floor of the cabin, repeating that he wasn't going to touch her, that he'd take her home as pure and chaste as when she left if only she'd stop crying.

She hadn't stopped, though, not once on the drive back to her parents' home. It was a wonder that Colin ever asked her for another date after that, much less asked her to marry him a few years later.

Kylie lifted a hand to brush the bittersweet memory away. That had happened in another lifetime, and she'd learned to handle situations with a little more finesse since then. Still, her sense of humor inserted, it might be good to keep in mind the shattering effect that hysterical tears had on a man—just in case sharing this house with Nick ever got out of her control.

"Plotting against me?" Nick asked as he moved from the shadows into the moonlight.

"Now, how did you guess?" Kylie didn't turn to look at him, knowing how attractive his off-center smile would be. "Don't tell me you've finished the dishes already?"

"Yes, no thanks to you. You could have helped dry, you know. Unless dishcloths also give you an allergic rash."

A low laugh rippled from her throat. "I could have helped, I suppose. But you did say we'd share the kitchen duty, and I didn't want to infringe on your turn."

"I'll remember that tomorrow night when it's your turn —allergic reaction or not."

"By this time tomorrow the automatic dishwasher will be fixed," she countered, swinging her feet to the ground and sitting on the edge of the chaise longue.

"And how are you going to arrange that? Don't tell me positive thinking works on appliances as well as employees?"

She tilted her chin and tried to disguise the smile that threatened the solemn line of her lips. "It's much simpler than that, Nick. I'll just ask Stephanie to take care of it for me."

His chuckle blended with the quietness around her. "Only one morning in the office and you've already learned the protocol of getting things done."

"It wasn't difficult. You made it obvious that Alex is president of Southwest Textiles in name only."

"I made it obvious?" Nick asked in a tone of disbelief.

"Of course you did. Alex is afraid to say his name in front of you because he's afraid you'll decide to change it."

"Don't be ridiculous. If it was left up to me, Alex could have carte blanche to do anything he wanted with the mill, and he knows it."

"Ah, the old sink or swim strategy," Kylie said, only half-teasing. "Alex sinks, and you swim right into his job as president."

Nick frowned heavily at her. "Not exactly. You see, Southwest is my Aunt Rosemary's pet project, and since Alex is her only son—*voilà*, a partnership made in heaven."

Kylie tried to distinguish some trace of rancor or resentment in the light sarcasm, but she couldn't be sure there was any hostility underlying his words. "And who appointed you guardian angel?"

He lifted his shoulders in a shrug. "I have strict orders from my grandfather to keep the company solvent, my aunt happy, and my cousin out of trouble. And, believe me, any one of the three can be a full-time job."

"It must be wonderful to be in business with your family. Very challenging."

"Very frustrating, most of the time." A slow smile creased his cheeks. "Actually I enjoy it. We're all pretty fond of each other, and there haven't been too many problems in resolving our differences. Of course, any discussion of business is strictly taboo at all family gatherings."

"But even at family gatherings I'll bet you sit at the head of the table."

"What difference does that make?" Nick drew a cigarette from his shirt pocket and cupped his hand against the slight breeze. In the brief flicker of the lighter she noted the lines of irritation around his mouth and smiled to herself. Almost instantly she felt his stern gaze fasten on her.

"Don't say it," he commanded. "I know smoking is a bad habit, and I don't need you to remind me."

Kylie couldn't hide her amusement. "You're very insecure, Nick. The thought never crossed my mind, and if it had, I wouldn't have been so rude as to say it aloud."

"Oh, I see. Now that I'm officially your employer, you're going to be careful about what you say to me."

"That's right, Nick. From this point on I intend to be a model prisoner. I mean employee. Sorry, just a slip of the tongue."

"Mmm-hmm, I'll bet." Nick slanted a considering look at her. "Kylie? May I ask you a personal question?"

Her heart jerked at the deep, almost suggestive tone of his voice. *Here it comes,* she thought. The stage was set for seduction with that enormous moon practically begging to be used for romance.

"Yes, I suppose so," she answered. Feeling a little like the fly about to enter the spider's parlor, Kylie stood and walked a few feet to the edge of the patio.

"Why did you break your engagement?"

Caught off guard, Kylie stiffened in automatic defensiveness. How had he known about that? "Engagement?"

She tried to marshal her thoughts as her brows arched upward questioningly.

"You shouldn't be surprised, Kylie. It was relatively simple to make inquiries about your company and you. Background checks are standard business procedure."

"Bad business procedure, Nick. Especially when you go beyond professional matters and pry into personal ones."

"You're in a position to influence my employees, Kylie. I wanted to know something about the people who have influenced you."

"I supplied references," she snapped, her fingernails imprinting her anger on the palm of her hand. "That was all . . . *all* . . . you had the right to check."

He looked coolly surprised at her irritation. "I'm afraid I have to disagree."

It was the height of arrogance, an intrusion she couldn't ignore. "If that's the way you feel, perhaps I should conduct an investigation into *your* background. After all, your influence on your employees is far greater than mine. It might be in the best interests of Southwest and my seminar for me to know something about the people who have influenced you." Kylie paused, letting the idea settle between them before she pushed for an apology. "Have you ever been engaged, Nick? Married? Divorced? Who was she? What was she like? Was she blond, brunette, or redheaded? Did she have blue eyes or br—?"

"Enough. You've made your point. I'm sorry that I offended you. I thought I had a valid reason." He hesitated as if he wasn't sure how she would react next. "Will it help if I admit that my reason was more personal than professional? I want to know more about you, Kylie."

A wry smile pestered her lips, and she sincerely hoped he couldn't see it. She should tell him to mind his own business, to stay out of her personal life, past and present. At any other time she would have done just that without

63

hesitation. But tonight she felt somehow alone. And Nick was perceptive enough to sense that, and to ask a personal question when she was in an unusually vulnerable mood.

Maybe it was the newness of her surroundings or the quiet solitude of the night. Perhaps it was simply the fragrance of memories in the air. Kylie sighed and knew she was going to tell him about Colin. "It wasn't my idea to break the engagement," she admitted. "Colin decided that for me. He married my best friend."

"I can't imagine you letting another woman take your fiancé without a fight."

"I wasn't much of a fighter then." Memories suddenly clouded her vision, and Kylie stared at a faraway star, thinking, remembering. She had never had to be a fighter, never had to make decisions. Colin had done that for her, and she had meekly accepted his right to be her guide and mentor. But then he had chosen to marry Susan. A woman with "spirit," Colin had said, a woman who knew what she wanted in life.

It had been a slap in the face, and Kylie had felt betrayed and hurt and afraid of having no one to depend on except herself. But in the months since, she had faced the fear and conquered it. She had discovered that she liked making her own decisions, liked the positive, assertive person she had learned to be.

"Kylie?"

At Nick's soft reminder of his presence the memories faded. "Sorry," she said. "I don't often talk about the past."

"Is it past, Kylie?" Nick seemed to hesitate before adding, "Or do you still love him?"

"No." She could say it easily now without even the tiniest twist of her heart. "Loving Colin was little more than a habit."

"Why does that make me want to smile?" Nick asked quietly, charging the air around her with electricity.

An ambience of intimacy enfolded her as her gaze covered the distance between them. In the dim light she couldn't see his expression, but she could feel their thoughts bonding in mutual understanding. His cigarette smoldered, a red-gold ember against the night, as something inside her caught and kindled into the first spark of desire.

Releasing her breath slowly, she made herself look away. "It happened a long time ago," she said to break the mood. "I hardly ever think about Colin anymore. There are still times when I miss Susan's friendship, though. Times when I'd like to telephone her, even though I know I can't. I know how awkward and uncomfortable we'd both feel."

The tightening in her throat choked back Kylie's words, and she had to blink moisture from her eyes. What was she doing? Talking to a near stranger about things she didn't even tell her family? Damn. She should have kept things strictly business with Nick. At least that was a mistake she could try to rectify. With cool composure she turned toward the house. "It's getting late. We should start working on the seminar."

Nick flicked his cigarette to the ground. His brows drew together in a puzzled line, as if he was startled by the sudden change in her manner. "There isn't any hurry. It's too beautiful a night to spend indoors working. Why don't we stay here and enjoy the company of that beautiful moon? We can relax and watch the stars play hide and seek with the wind."

The courtly charm of his words irritated Kylie unreasonably. It was too late now for Nick to notice the moon and the aura of romance around them, she thought. If he'd

just had the good sense to steer clear of personal questions.
. . .

"Mr. Braden," she snapped, more out of frustration than anything else, "I'm here to give a six-week seminar which *you* have cut to three weeks. I don't have time to waste on romantic drivel!" Kylie pressed her lips together and walked toward the house, knowing that the last thing she wanted to do was work on the seminar. With an exasperated sigh she pulled open the door and went inside.

Nick frowned as the door closed behind her. He drew a cigarette from his pocket and tapped it impatiently against his palm. *Romantic drivel.* The words chafed his male vanity, and he tossed the cigarette aside in disgust.

Damnation! Why was he so fascinated by her? He'd known plenty of women as physically attractive, and not one of them had had such a volatile temperament.

Kylie Richards was argumentative, illogical, fiercely independent, and totally frustrating. Nick shoved his hands into the back pockets of his jeans and stared at the silhouette of the Sangre de Cristo Mountains. Frustrating or not, he couldn't deny that something about Kylie captivated him; some elusive quality that he glimpsed at odd moments behind the challenge of her dark eyes. He sensed a softness, a vulnerability in her, and he knew he wouldn't be satisfied until he'd discovered the secret of her appeal.

He thought of her fiancé and all that Kylie had left unsaid. She had been deeply hurt by that broken engagement, and Nick wished he could tell the man to his face what an inconsiderate fool—

Recognizing the intensity of his feelings, Nick stopped and distanced himself from the emotion. Analytically he examined his sudden violent dislike for the unknown Colin and had to admit there was no logic involved. Just as there was no logical reason for wishing he'd known

Kylie then, when he might have been able to protect her from the hurt.

Nick ran restless fingers through his hair. He must be out of his mind! She ranked right beside Mata Hari when it came to needing a man's protection. Kylie would resent it, and he had little doubt she'd tell him so, too, without a minute's hesitation.

Gazing thoughtfully at the house, he made a decision. A decision that had been forming in his mind since she had calmly and defiantly challenged him in the restaurant. Kylie was going to be his, no matter how assertive she was. He'd bide his time, but he would master that streak of defiance in her. Even if he had to give her the extra three weeks for her ridiculous seminar.

Stifling a yawn, Kylie tried to concentrate on the scribbled notes in her hand. It was impossible to decipher the last few lines, she decided with a surreptitious glance at Nick. He wasn't watching her, and she took a minute to notice how the blue of his polo shirt changed the color of his eyes. His lashes were dark and thick, but utterly masculine. But, then, everything about Nick was forcefully male. Even the lazy way he was sitting. With his arms stretched along the back of the sofa and his feet propped on the coffee table, he looked disgustingly at ease.

Kylie flexed her legs cautiously and tried to find a more comfortable position on the carpeted floor. Her fingers ached from taking down the pages of notes Nick had dictated, information he was certain she'd need.

If he hadn't been so polite ever since they'd come inside the house, she might have called it a day more than an hour ago. But as long as he stopped every now and then to ask her in a patient and considerate tone whether she needed him to repeat something, she was determined to match him in endurance if nothing else.

With a concerted effort she forced the pen across the paper but knew she was too far behind to catch up. There was nothing to do now except to admit defeat gracefully and retreat to her room for the night. Nick would be understanding. In fact, she fully expected him to tell her that she looked as if she needed the rest and he would have stopped dictating a long time before if he'd known she was tired.

Kylie tightened her lips to a narrow line, knowing she was being unreasonably annoyed by Nick's charm, but unable to conquer the feeling. At the moment, she would far prefer a down-to-earth argument than this walking-on-eggs type of treatment.

What was he trying to do to her, anyway? Wear down her resistance with soft looks and smiles? Alex wasn't the only one who could turn on the charisma, she thought. And, as in everything else, Nick seemed to do it so much better.

Kylie began drawing flowers on her note pad and let Nick's voice provide the accompaniment to her thoughts. She wondered idly if Nick was like his cousin in any other ways. As far as she knew, Nick could have a live-in blonde waiting back in San Francisco. Somehow she didn't think so, but she supposed it was possible. He might be simply looking for a diversion to pass the time while he was in New Mexico.

She wrote the name *Nick* on the pad, then scratched through it and printed *Alex.* At the thought of Alex, her gaze shifted to the bouquet of yellow roses on the coffee table before her. Two dozen roses made an exquisite centerpiece, she decided. Noticing that one rose looked slightly droopy, she reached for it.

"I'm ready to quit any time you are," Nick said, cutting into her thoughts with droll humor.

68

A thorn stabbed her finger, and she jerked back to frown intently at him.

His smile was easy and amused. "You should always be very careful with floral offerings from secret admirers. When a man sends an excess of roses, you can be pretty sure he's up to no good."

Kylie widened her eyes in pretended innocence. "Is that right? Tell me, Nick, when you send roses, are you up to no good?"

"Every single time."

Fighting a smile, she tilted her head to one side. "Well, I believe I can handle your cousin without too much trouble."

"Alex?" Nick asked, a sharp edge fraying his smooth voice. "Alex sent these? Why would he send you flowers?"

Her brows arched upward in a haughty angle. "For the usual reasons, of course. He's obviously up to no good."

Nick paused, wondering how he could get his foot out of his mouth this time. The thought of Alex and Kylie together made him uncomfortable, but he knew he was simply imagining things. Alex had probably sent the roses because . . . Nick couldn't think of a single platonic reason for such extravagance and finally gave himself a mental shake. He *was* imagining things. Kylie would never be fooled by Alex's effusive tactics.

Nick tried a disarming grin. "You're not planning to change your hair color, are you?"

"What makes you think I'd have to do that, Nick? Alex might think he prefers blondes, but it wouldn't take much effort to change his mind if I wanted to."

"But you don't want to," Nick stated confidently.

Kylie carefully pulled the droopy rose from the vase and held it in her hand. "I didn't say that. It might be quite a challenge. Would you like to make a small wager that by the end of this seminar Alex won't be wondering what he ever saw in his succession of mindless blondes?"

Nick looked suddenly as if he wanted to jerk the rose from her fingers, but when he spoke, his tone was casual. "I can't accept your wager, Kylie. That would be taking unfair advantage of you. Believe me, you won't change his mind, and it wouldn't be worth the trouble to try, just to win a bet."

Nick was right about that, Kylie thought as she studied the velvety petals of the rose. Alex wouldn't be worth the trouble. "Well, we'll just have to see what happens, won't we?" she said absently. "I think I'll call it a night. Good night, Nick." She walked to the doorway, already anticipating the release of the evening's tension in a hot bath.

Nick's gaze fell from the doorway directly onto the note pad and the sight of his name marked through a half dozen times. He circled the coffee table to examine the pad more carefully. But there was no mistake. Kylie had written his name and then boldly slashed through it—not once but several times.

Alex's name wasn't marked that way, he noticed. In fact, Alex's name was encircled by a wreath of flowers. A flash of unreasonable jealousy raced through Nick as he turned a suspicious eye on the bouquet of roses. If Kylie thought for one minute that she and Alex . . .

Before he quite knew his intention, Nick was standing outside her bedroom door. With a peremptory knock he opened the door and stepped inside.

Startled, Kylie whirled to face him, making an inadequate attempt to cover her breasts with one hand as she grabbed frantically with the other for the blouse she'd just discarded.

"Nick! What are you doing?" Her groping fingers fastened on the soft material, and she jerked it up to cover herself, realizing too late that she'd pulled the coverlet from the bed. Angry embarrassment flooded her cheeks with hot color as she tried to adjust the bulky satin spread around her. When she focused her attention on Nick, though, the embarrassment gave way to a different type of heat.

The smoldering appraisal in his eyes took her breath away, and for a pulsebeat her fingers relaxed their grip. But as the satiny material began to ease down the curve of her breasts, Kylie recognized the danger and clutched the makeshift wrapper to stop its willful descent. With as much dignity and poise as she could manage, Kylie squared her shoulders and tipped her chin.

"You'd better have a good reason for barging in here like this," she stated, trying to recapture her initial angry response.

"I did, but I think I just forgot what it was." His gaze slid slowly upward, lingering at the base of her throat and caressing her bare shoulders before singeing her lips with its intensity. "You know, Kylie, you look extraordinarily lovely in a bedspread."

Her lips pursed in a line of irritation. "Thank you. It's the latest style for those times when a man walks uninvited into your bedroom."

"What's the style when he's invited?"

Hitching the coverlet higher, she glared at him, vacillating between annoyance and sensual awareness. "If you don't know the answer to that question, Nick," she challenged, "maybe you should ask Alex for some pointers."

Immediately Nick's expression grew stern, and he scanned the room with ill-concealed impatience. Kylie watched, mystified, as he walked to the dresser, lifted the rose she'd placed there, and turned to face her.

"This is the reason I barged *uninvited* into your room." His voice was low but unmistakably determined as he dropped the yellow rose into the trash receptacle. "You

71

may as well understand right now, Kylie, that nothing is going to happen between you and my cousin. No wager, no relationship—nothing is going to happen with Alex. Do you hear me?"

"Loud and clear," she snapped. "And now I'd like to hear why you feel this chauvinistic display of authority is necessary. Are you afraid that with my help Alex might gain a little authority of his own? Maybe even pose a threat to your job?"

"Job?" Nick asked with a puzzled lift of his brows. "What does my job have to do with this?"

"Alex said enough about the situation for me to know that the two of you are involved in some executive power struggle. But if you think for one minute that I'm—"

"Kylie, this has nothing to do with my job or Alex's. I want to be sure you have no plans to change his mind about women in general and blondes in particular." Nick's gaze held hers with unyielding strength. "I won't allow it."

Her own determination rose to meet his. Nick might as well understand right now that she had no intention of following this or any other order from him. "If that's what I want to do, Nick, then you won't stop me from doing it."

He drew in his breath sharply. "Kylie, we are going to be lovers, and once that happens, you won't have the time or inclination to think about Alex or any other man."

Kylie grappled with his words. "We?" she whispered hoarsely. "As in you and me?"

"We," Nick clarified. "As in you and I. *We* are going to be lovers."

Her lips parted on a stunned gasp. "You must be out of your mind." But her thoughts reeled in dizzy circles, already considering the idea. Nick as her lover? One part of her rejected his statement as nonsense, as an attempt to

72

dominate her. But another part of her trembled with the knowledge that he wanted her, for whatever reason. "You *are* out of your mind," she repeated.

"We'll just have to see what happens, won't we?" His lips curved in a confident smile. "I think I'd better leave before it becomes necessary to prove to you that I'm quite sane." He walked to the door, then turned. "On second thought, this has all happened rather suddenly. Maybe we both need some proof." He advanced toward her, purpose in every movement.

Kylie took one step back and hugged the coverlet to her like a security blanket. But it offered little protection when Nick placed his hands on her bare shoulders and pulled her into his arms.

She struggled with the shivers of anticipation that cascaded down her spine. *This is a time for resistance,* she told herself sternly as his lips brushed hers and lingered with irresistible softness. With a will of its own her mouth moved beneath his, accepting his touch and denying her caution. Kylie wondered vaguely why she didn't break free of his hold, but somehow that seemed the wrong way to meet this new and unexpected challenge.

His hand traced caressing circlets across her back as he reluctantly raised his head. "Soon, Kylie," he murmured. "Soon."

By the time he reached the doorway a second time, she had rediscovered her voice and a subdued measure of irritation. "I'm not impressed by these—these caveman tactics, Nick."

His dark eyebrows arched in skeptical amusement. "I guess I'll have to try a different approach then, won't I? Good night, Kylie. Try not to dream of me." With a soft click the door closed behind him.

His words echoed through her thoughts like a tantalizing melody. An irritatingly persistent melody that wouldn't go away. *Try not to dream of me.* Not a chance now that she wouldn't.

Over and over, as she undressed and ran a bath, his words came back to her. *We're going to be lovers.* Lovers. Her mind conjured up images of Nick's virile strength possessing her body. Her fingers curled into her palms as she wondered how his bare skin would feel against hers. Smooth, she thought, but with a texture that would excite and stimulate her senses. His lips would explore her, discover her in a thousand sensual ways. Nick would be a tender, sensitive lover, and she—

Kylie began to hum tunelessly to dispel the images. She must be out of her mind to consider it at all. No matter how attracted she was to Nick, she had to remember the dangers he presented. He was used to being in control of situations and of people. If she let herself get involved with him, he'd try to mold her to his will, take charge of her life, all the things that she'd promised herself would never happen to her again.

It had taken too long to achieve the confidence and self-assurance she now had; she wouldn't let Nick threaten her newfound independence. Not that she had any idea how she'd manage to resist his appealing lopsided smile, but she'd find a way. And somehow, even if she had to stay awake all night, she wouldn't dream of him either.

Closing her eyes, she sank up to her chin in the warm water of the bath. It promised to be a very long night.

CHAPTER FOUR

In the days that followed, Kylie told herself that the scene in her bedroom had been an absurd dream, a ridiculous flight of imagination. For a week and a half, Nick did nothing to discredit her theory. In fact, she often thought he couldn't possibly have been more charming.

During the training sessions and over dinner Nick was courteous, attentive, and friendly. He was businesslike and professional during the evenings, giving her information on the plant and employees. But always the evenings ended as the grandfather clock in the hall chimed eleven, ended with a cordial good-night that would have restored the faith of the most anxious mother. In every way Nick proved himself a perfect gentleman, and Kylie vacillated between feelings of confused relief and irrational pique.

It wasn't fair, she decided on Thursday morning as she listened to the expectant hum of voices in the cafeteria-turned-auditorium. She should be concentrating on the morning's lecture or any number of other important things, but her thoughts centered increasingly on Nick.

Day and night he was a tiny paper cut in her mind, an annoying ache that simply wouldn't leave her alone.

"Here's the data sheet you wanted." Stephanie extended the page for Kylie's inspection.

Blinking aside thoughts of Nick, Kylie scanned the list and nodded. "Can we have copies for everyone by tomorrow—early?"

"No problem." Stephanie looked over the crowded room, her blue eyes seeking and hopeful. "He'll be here today, Kylie. I made a point to remind him this morning."

Kylie knew there was only one "he" who rated that wistful note in Stephanie's voice. Alex had a perfect record of absence at the sessions, but his secretary seemed certain that would change at any moment.

It wasn't fair. Kylie returned to her original conclusion as she gathered together her notes and approached the podium. Stephanie wanted Alex here, and Kylie wished Nick was anywhere else. Placing her notes on the stand, she looked to the back of the room.

He was there, of course, in the same chair, in the same corner of the room that he occupied during each and every session, impeccably dressed and looking impossibly handsome. In the artificial light his hair glinted like the patina of polished wood. His dark brows were a shadowy emphasis over eyes of indeterminate expression. Distance made the contours of his face indefinite, but she knew the chiseled lines by memory, knew how they firmed with determination and gentled with laughter. He caught her glance and smiled.

Lovers, Kylie, soon. Right on cue his words were in her mind again. Just as they always were when he smiled at her or touched her hand in a casual way that somehow didn't seem casual at all. It just wasn't fair.

She focused her attention on the assembled employees. "Good morning. It's time to begin."

As an interested hush fell over the room Kylie shoved Nick to the far corners of her mind and paused to let her confidence build. Here at least she knew she was in charge. Despite Nick, despite Alex, despite numerous little problems the seminar was going beautifully, and that fact alone was sweet satisfaction.

"Today I'm going to present some suggestions on setting realistic goals and the positive steps you can take toward achieving them. Then we'll divide into discussion groups. Any questions? Good, let's get started."

The morning sped to a hurried lunch, consisting of salad, a soft drink, and a perusal of the afternoon training material. It was past three o'clock before Kylie, with Stephanie at her side, opened the door of her tiny office and sank into the only chair.

"Sorry I can't offer you a place to sit." Kylie kicked off her navy leather pumps and wearily massaged her feet. "My request for another chair must have gotten hijacked on its way to your office."

"It's probably buried somewhere on Alex's desk. I'll check before I leave, even though I don't look forward to seeing the paper work that's accumulated since this morning." Stephanie wrinkled her pert nose. "It's nice to feel needed, but sometimes I think he really couldn't manage without me. In the office, anyway."

"Alex certainly depends on you to keep his life running smoothly."

"Oh, he depends on me all right, but for all the wrong reasons." Stephanie leaned against the desk and traced fingertip designs on the top. "I never intended to be a—a fixture in his life. When I first started working for him, it was different. But now he seems to think I'm just part of the office equipment. Something for his convenience. He takes advantage of me, you know."

77

Kylie did know, but she simply nodded since Stephanie didn't give her a chance to speak.

"I've always hoped that one day he'd realize . . . " Stephanie let the thought drift into a pensive silence ending with a half-embarrassed smile. "Do you mind if I take home your notes from today's session? I'd like to look over them again, if it's all right."

Hesitating just long enough to catch up with the change of subject, Kylie retrieved the notes and handed them across the desk. "Be my guest if you're sure you want to spend your evening that way."

"Oh, I do. I want to learn as much about assertiveness principles as I can." Stephanie paused for a thoughtful moment. "Kylie? Do you really believe in setting goals and working toward them?"

"Yes, of course. It's the only way to achieve the things you want."

Stephanie looked at the pages in her hand as if she'd just discovered a wonderful secret. "I'll bet you set personal goals, too, don't you? I mean, things you want for yourself. Like a new car or a different job or—well, you know, *personal* goals."

Suddenly wary of the resourceful gleam in the blue eyes, Kylie tempered her response. "Almost anything, personal or not, requires planning and taking some positive action toward getting it."

"The same principles apply, don't they?"

Kylie hesitated. "Basically, yes. But—"

There was a rough knock on the door, and Nick stepped into the office. The room seemed almost diminutive inundated by his presence. In the space of a heartbeat Kylie noticed everything about him: his long legs, which carried him with lithe grace; the effortless fit of his jacket over his powerful shoulders and arms; his dark hair, combed, then touseled by his careless fingers; his expressive brows,

78

which slanted a greeting her way; his gray eyes, reflecting a smile that accentuated that mesmerizing cleft in his chin. The scent of him tickled her senses, and she nestled more securely into the chair.

"Hello," she said, ignoring the disgraceful flutter in her throat.

"Good afternoon, ladies." Nick advanced into the room and seated himself on the corner of the desk closest to Kylie. She felt the brush of his trouser leg whisper against her nylon-clad calf, and a current of sensation swirled leisurely through her. Against her will she lowered her gaze to the source of the delicate sensation; she knew he was watching, for his lips twitched with a smile. "Is this a private party," he asked, "or may I join you?"

"Considering that you already seem reasonably settled in, please join us." Kylie made a pretense of smoothing her stocking before she looked up. "Take your shoes off and make yourself comfortable. Stephanie and I were just discussing the lavish furnishings of my office."

Nick sent a cursory glance around the cubicle. "Nice. You have a real flair for life's basics, Kylie. A desk, chair, and pencils. You've really done wonders with this room."

"Why, thank you, Mr. Braden. Just think what I could do if I had, say, another three weeks?" Extra time for the seminar was a dead issue, but Kylie liked to remind him now and then that he wasn't giving her a fair chance.

Nick gave a doubtful shake of his head. "I don't see how you could improve on this. What do you think, Stephanie?"

"I think I should plead the fifth amendment," Stephanie answered lightly, "before you decide I should redecorate my office."

Nick's chuckle tugged a response from Kylie. As their eyes met to share the lighthearted teasing the sheer force of his masculinity sent a jolt through her. The room seemed to become suffocatingly close and then to expand oddly.

A movement from Stephanie restored perspective. "Thanks for the use of these, Kylie." Stephanie lifted the notes for emphasis. "I'd better check in with—"

"Well, finally," Alex drawled from the doorway, immediately gaining everyone's attention. His appearance was immaculate, from the tip of his leather oxfords to the careful styling of his blond hair. "Do you know I've been all over the plant looking for you?" He gave Stephanie a mildly reproachful look. "The training session ended thirty minutes ago, and there's some correspondence on my desk that has to be mailed tonight. Do you think you could manage to get it done before midnight?"

Kylie thought of a dozen snappy replies, but Stephanie stayed painfully quiet, although her chin lifted a fraction.

"Hello, Alex," Nick said pointedly. "So nice to see you."

"Cousin." Alex bent his head in slight acknowledgment before he moved purposely past Nick to Kylie's side. He took her hand and raised it to his lips for a suave kiss. "Hello, Kylie."

"Hello, Alex." She firmly pulled her hand from his grasp. "Did you come looking for Stephanie or just to impress me with your manners?"

The sarcasm was lost on his overblown ego. "I came to request the pleasure of your company at a prestigious party tomorrow night. Are you free for the evening?"

What gall! He asks as if there could be no question of my desire to be his date, she thought as a dozen satisfying ways to refuse came to mind.

"Sorry, Cousin," Nick said. "You're too late. Kylie's attending the party with me."

"She is?" Alex frowned at Nick in exasperation. "Well,

what am I supposed to do? Everyone knows you can't go stag to one of Glynnis Claybrook's parties."

Kylie decided to accept Nick's interference as a momentary godsend and to argue with him later, after she'd enjoyed Alex's rare discomfort. "What happened to Miss —your roommate?"

"She moved to Las Vegas." Alex provided the information with a shrug. "We didn't have much in common anyway. I like women with a little more spirit, like you, Kylie. Why don't we find Nick another date, and then you'll be free to go with me? I'm younger and much more fun." Alex glanced around the room as if searching for someone to serve as Nick's date. He passed over Stephanie's still form as if she didn't exist. "I'm sure we can find someone for him."

Nick's smile became more determined. "I have a date, Alex. Find someone for yourself."

"Oh, be a sport, Nick," Alex cajoled. "Who could I ask at the last minute? You can't expect me to go with just anyone, you know." He paused, as if mentally reviewing potential candidates. "Well, I'll think of someone." With a dismissing sigh he turned to his secretary. "Oh, Bunny, that reminds me. I meant to ask you. Would you—"

"Why, thank you, Alex," Stephanie said with a level stare that by rights should have frozen him in his tracks. "I'd love to go with you to the party tomorrow night."

In the stunned silence that followed, Stephanie squared her shoulders and tilted her chin defiantly. The notes in her hand made a faintly ominous rustle. "As for tonight, I'll get as much of the correspondence done as I can before five o'clock, Alex, but I'm not working any later." She pivoted and walked from the room.

Kylie controlled the impish quiver of her lips and watched as one emotion after another altered Alex's features. He couldn't have looked more astounded.

"Did I just ask *Bunny* to the party?"

"Congratulations," Nick offered. "You not only asked but were accepted."

"I can't believe it." Alex whispered the words in disbelief. "And she called me Alex. I can't imagine what's gotten into her."

Kylie had a pretty good idea. Nick obviously had the same thought, for the arch of his brows emphasized his conclusion. "Yes," he said dryly, "it's hard to imagine."

Kylie tried to look suitably mystified. With a bemused shake of his head Alex lifted a hand in farewell and walked from the room.

As Nick shifted his position on the desk Kylie tensed, anticipating the brush of his leg against hers. It didn't come, but she felt that same intangible current of sensation, as if he had touched her. She moved slightly, placing her legs out of touching range, real or imagined.

"How long do you think it will take Alex to break that date?" she asked.

"I don't think he's going to get the opportunity. Stephanie appears to be in control of the situation, and with some extra coaching from you there'll be no end to the upheaval she'll create in Alex's life."

"Extra coaching?" Kylie echoed. Irritation welled up in her, its source as much what Nick had said as the perpetual amusement in his eyes. "Stephanie has had the same training as every other employee, no more and no less. She just has the good sense to listen. Unlike you, Nick."

"I listen to every word that passes your lips, Kylie."

"And you don't take any of them seriously."

His smile was slow and disarming. "I take you very seriously. Would you like me to show you?" He stood, then fluidly bent beside her chair until his gaze was level with hers. His thumb began to etch feathery circles on the back of her hand.

Kylie melted a little deeper into her chair before she rallied. "If you're thinking of kissing my hand, I'll warn you that I'm not impressed by that sort of thing."

"You're not?" He slipped his fingers beneath hers, cradling the smallness of her hand in his. For a breathless second he focused all his attention on lifting her hand to his lips. But just as her skin tingled with expectation he stopped.

Then slowly, ever so slowly he turned her hand until his breath warmed and tantalized her palm. Like an autumn leaf Kylie hung suspended, waiting for his touch. When at last he pressed his mouth against her sensitive flesh, a tremulous sigh spread throughout her body.

The sensuous flick of his tongue robbed her of coherent thought before he raised his eyes and caught her in his gaze.

Kylie knew she looked impressed, but she couldn't seem to help herself. With exaggerated care Nick placed her hand in her lap. "Alex never was very good at that sort of thing."

She faltered over the catch in her throat and finally found her voice. "Sometimes it's hard to believe the two of you are related."

"I think that's the nicest thing you've ever said to me." Nick feigned a suspicious frown. "You're not trying to get out of fixing dinner tonight, are you?"

"I wouldn't dream of it. What would you like to have?"

It was the pause—the merest breath of a hesitation—as much as the tilt of his smile that gave her the answer. He wanted her. The knowledge closed around her with bewitching surety and firmed her fluctuating resolve to resist. "I'll settle for steak and salad," he said.

"You bet you will."

Surprise played across his face just seconds before a

laugh flowed deep and rich from his throat. "Always a step ahead of me, aren't you?"

"Always," she lied. "You should keep that in mind."

With a noncommittal twitch of his mouth he straightened and moved around the desk to the doorway. "I'll see you this evening, Kylie." It was a husky promise, and with it he was gone.

To keep from staring at the doorway, Kylie glanced around her office and wondered why it no longer seemed devoid of character. But there was no denying that it felt different. No denying that it held the essence of Nick's laughter, the lingering warmth of his presence.

And there was no doubt that she was getting involved with Nick Braden. She had all the symptoms. The fluttery pulse, the sudden inexplicable smiles, the daydreams. It was all too familiar. She'd fallen in and out of love before, and she knew it was a quicksilver emotion that came and went without explanation.

Only with Colin it had been different. He'd been the handsome older man who'd waited on the sidelines of her life for her to grow into love for him. He had taken control of her young plans and dreams and then left her devastatingly empty when he'd turned to someone with "more spirit."

More spirit. That still haunted her. Even after all this time. Even after she'd pulled herself together and discovered her own brand of spirit.

And now she was trembling on the brink of another relationship. One that intrigued her and yet threatened the independence she'd fought so hard to acquire. Of course Nick was different from Colin. More mature, more understanding. But she'd be a fool to ignore the similarities: the determination, the strength of purpose.

Kylie loosened the combs that held her chestnut hair and let its weight fall to her shoulders. It was all laid out like a chessboard, ready for one of them to make a move. And she knew she would have to make a decision soon before the option to decide was taken from her control. Already Nick was making decisions that involved her on one level or another.

Oh, he was skilled at this game, she admitted, staring wryly at her still-tingling palm. Without crossing the bounds of propriety he was seducing her.

Correction, she thought. Nick had merely planted the idea. She had done the rest.

Mentally snapping her fingers, Kylie forced her attention to the work at hand. She'd worked hard for this seminar, too hard to spend any more time daydreaming about Nick. As she began to prepare the next day's lecture her heart, undaunted by logic, lightened with anticipation of the evening ahead.

It was the absence of workaday sounds that finally broke her concentration. A glance at her watch prompted a groan and a hurried attempt to put her desk in order. After six o'clock. Nick would think—Her mad rush came to a screeching halt. What Nick would think was immaterial. There was nothing in her contract about cooking, but there was plenty about the quality of the seminar she would give.

Leisurely Kylie completed her work. She drove to the house at the same unhurried pace. Just let him say one word, she thought, her defenses primed and ready, as she pushed open the front door and stepped inside.

The first word was hers, though, as she noticed the shimmer of candlelight on china and the appetizing aroma. The table was set for two, and a feeling of intimacy pervaded the room as Nick came through the kitchen doorway. He was dressed in jeans and a knit shirt, and his smile was just as casual. His appearance and manner were

85

the same as on any other night, but something was different. She could feel it.

In an instant Kylie assessed the situation and knew there would be no discussion of seminars tonight. She had the fleeting impression of a chess piece moving irrevocably, inevitably toward decision.

CHAPTER FIVE

Kylie camouflaged her uncertainty with a challenging lift of her chin. "I'm late."

Nick's thumb stroked the line of his jaw. "It's hard to argue with that, but I get the feeling I'm supposed to."

"Don't be silly. I make it a practice never to argue before dinner."

"Good, because I'm hungry." He moved to the table and drew back her chair with an elaborate gesture. "But don't think I've forgotten that it was really your turn to cook. You owe me, Kylie, and I intend to collect."

Halfway into the chair she jerked around to bring him into her line of vision and almost missed the seat. He braced her with a hand at her waist that brushed seductively against her breast as he settled her. Obviously she hadn't imagined the innuendo in his voice, but she could ignore it. She made a production of placing her napkin in her lap. "You're obsessed with food, Nick."

His breath fanned the curls at her temple before reaching her ear. "It keeps me from dwelling on more delectable delights."

"Oh, does that mean you made dessert too?" It was a weak comeback, but she excused it as being made under duress and pretended a starving interest in the food before her. "Ummm. Steak and salad. This looks good, Nick. You must have spent hours—"

Nick seated himself at the table and silenced her with a look. "Just eat, Kylie."

She obeyed, feeling oddly more relaxed. There was no reason to overreact, to assume this night would be different from any other. She could handle Nick. After all, he couldn't seduce her without her cooperation, could he?

She made a considerable dent in her dinner before the silence became uncomfortable. "Were you in Alex's office tonight?" she asked. "Did Stephanie leave at five?"

"On the dot. You should have seen Alex's face."

"Good for her. Alex has had it coming for a long time. Stephanie just needed to gain a little confidence and self-respect."

"She may have to gain new employment."

Kylie's eyes widened. "He wouldn't dare fire her!" Nick didn't offer a response as he sipped his coffee, and another thought occurred to Kylie. "*You* wouldn't fire her, would you?"

"I might." He stopped her protest with a gesture. "Southwest can't afford a defiance of authority. Not in the executive office."

"Defiance? Stephanie is only asserting her rights."

"There's a fine line between assertiveness and rebellion, Kylie. And I didn't say I was going to fire her, I just sai—"

"Haven't you listened to anything I've said during the training? Stephanie has just discovered that she isn't an automaton to be plugged in and turned off at the company, or Alex's, convenience. Employees deserve to be treated as an important and necessary part of the business they work for."

88

"I agree in principle, Kylie, but—"

"You're so entrenched in your master and slave theories of management that—"

"Master and slave?" His eyes flickered a disgruntled warning. "You're exaggerating. But let's talk about something else. I don't want to argue toni—"

"We're not arguing. I'm just telling you that you don't know what it's like not to have a voice in the everyday decisions that concern you. You've never had someone make all the decisions for you."

"And you have, I suppose?"

"Yes. Colin used to—" Realizing that somehow the conversation had become personal, Kylie sought a way to change it. "I understand how Stephanie feels, Nick. There was a time when I did what I was told because I didn't believe in my ability to think for myself. Certainly office rules must be followed. But assertiveness training doesn't advocate breaking rules. It simply teaches you to respect the rights of others and to expect the same consideration for your own rights."

"You're very convincing, Kylie." He leaned forward to cover her hand with his.

She heard the skepticism in his voice. "But you're not convinced, are you, Nick?"

"No," he conceded with a heavy sigh. "But couldn't we just agree to disagree? After all, what's a little disagreement between—friends?"

"Nothing at all." She snatched her hand from his touch and pushed back from the table. "I'll take care of the dishes. You can practice cracking your whip."

His silence was expressive as she stood and began stacking the plates and silverware. "Kylie, I—" He paused and seemed to come to a decision. "How about a rousing game of Scrabble?"

A fork clattered against the plate as she looked to see if he was joking. "Scrabble?" she echoed. "I'd beat you."

"Doesn't that appeal to you at the moment?" He smiled, and she was irritated by his attempt at persuasion.

"You're on, Nick. But no cheating."

He raised his right hand in solemn denial. "The dictionary and I will be waiting."

After clearing the table and loading the dishwasher Kylie slipped to her bedroom to change clothes. She exchanged the tailored shirtwaist dress for jeans and a blue checked blouse, combed her hair, then promptly mussed the curls into disorder again. She would make no concessions to whatever amorous plans Nick might have for the evening. Amorous plans, she thought and made a face at her reflection. If previous evenings in his company were any indication, his only advance would be to spell a suggestive word on the Scrabble board.

That was cold comfort, though, especially when she entered the living room and saw Nick. He looked up from his prone position on the floor, propped himself up on an elbow, and motioned for her to join him. It was a casual gesture, but her pulse skipped at the grace of his movements. She veiled her inspection of the sensuous length of his body and lowered herself to sit cross-legged opposite him.

With feigned concentration on the game set out between them, she chose seven letter tiles. She tried to ignore his disquieting appraisal and wondered why her resistance seemed to be ebbing away. Finally she met the seductive amusement in his eyes with a guileless smile. "Your move, Mr. Braden."

"Yes, it is, isn't it?" he answered, his tone of voice making it clear that his words had a double meaning. He placed two letters on the game board and recorded his score.

Kylie looked at his word, *is,* then at her letter tiles, then back to the board. A frown grooved a dimple in her cheek as she realized she had only one playing option. With a show of nonchalance she picked two letters and formed the word *kiss.*

"Good start," he commented as he counted her points.

It wasn't a good start, though, and as the game progressed it went from bad to worse. Her points accumulated steadily, but so did the suggestive words. *Ouch* became *touch, at* became *pat.* When she tried to cheat and make the word *beed,* Nick called illegal procedure, and she had to shorten it to *bed.*

The play continued until she was left with an *s,* which would only fit in front of his *ex.* She accused him of using a prefix as a word, and while he leafed through the dictionary she discarded the remaining letter and totaled the scores.

"I won," she announced.

"Oh, no, you didn't." He gave her a quelling look. "*Ex,* as a word, is listed at least four times. You're not playing fair, and I demand a rematch."

"You should learn to accept defeat gracefully, Nick."

"It seems pointless when it happens so seldom."

Her gaze traced the line of his jaw but found no hint of arrogance. He simply didn't often lose, even at games of Scrabble. "Of course," she teased, "that was before you met me."

She moved her legs to stretch her cramped muscles before reclining full length on the carpet. Too late Kylie realized the unconscious invitation of her position, but she knew that jerking upright would be even more incriminating. So she closed her eyes and hoped Nick wouldn't notice her vulnerability.

Subtle and seemingly almost reluctant as it was, a man would have to be blind not to notice that invitation, Nick

91

decided. And he wasn't blind when it came to Kylie. He watched the lifting thrust of her breasts as she breathed and knew the familiar ache of desire. His hand, of its own volition, reached toward her, stopped, and with a betraying tremble returned to his side. Masking a sigh, he rolled onto his back and stared at the beamed ceiling.

She was close. Too close. And he wanted like hell to toss reason on its ear and make love to her. It wouldn't be difficult. She wasn't immune to desire. Even now the silence fairly vibrated with awareness. All he had to do was turn and kiss her the way he'd wanted to kiss her for days on end.

Frustration at his own weakness knotted his stomach. It wasn't that simple at all. He wanted the pleasure of her body, but more than that he wanted her soft and yielding in his arms. He wanted to capture her laughter and replace the rebellious gleam in her eyes with a smile—just for him.

And she would come to him that way if he gave her time. His hands-off strategy had worked so far. He knew she recognized the attraction between them, and she hadn't done anything to discourage it. At the moment that was small satisfaction, but he'd promised himself that he wouldn't rush her.

"Kylie? What do you want most in life?" Nick hated the trite question, but he had to do something to keep from touching her, didn't he?

"Hmmm." She mulled the question over before answering. "My immediate objective is to make you admit you were wrong about the seminar. I want you to say, on bended knee of course, 'Kylie, I see the error of my ways, and I apologize for being so bullheaded, opinionated, and —"

"I thought you believed in setting *realistic* goals."

Her laugh was musical, and Nick resolutely closed his mind against its siren call.

"After I convince you and finish the training here, I'll track down another lead and find someone willing to listen and give Motivation Management a chance. Maybe one day companies will be waiting in line for my seminars."

"With your persistence I'm sure you'll succeed."

"Do you think so? The thought scares me silly." She raised herself on an elbow and turned toward him. "I suppose I shouldn't admit that to you."

"Why not? I can be as understanding as anyone else. Reaching a goal you've set for yourself can be frightening because then you have to set new ones."

The air seemed full of unspoken thoughts and dreams that oddly didn't need a voice. Without warning he felt the gentle stroke of her finger on his chin, and his resolve crumbled. His hand closed over her wrist, and he pulled her down on top of him. He knew this lapse would probably bring regret later, but for now he had to have a taste, just a taste of her lips.

Hesitation hung between them like a separate presence, and Kylie could only stare into the cloudy depths of his eyes. She had instigated his action unintentionally, but she knew she couldn't tease him by resisting. She didn't want to resist. Or tease. But she was so very unsure of herself with Nick, unsure, but absolutely certain she had to feel his kiss. Her doubts succumbed to temptation, and a sigh escaped her lips as she lowered her mouth to his.

The touch was zephyr soft and melted into her like the first drops of a gentle rain. And, thirsty for him, she returned for another taste. And another, until his hand cupped her nape and urged her to drink more deeply.

It was a lovely, delicate meeting of lips that made her glad she was a woman and could discover pleasure in his kiss, in his quiescent strength beneath her fingertips. It was a feeling of power and, at the same time, a reminder of her own weakness—a give and take that required surrender but promised a thousand delights.

He parted her lips with tender insistence, and a silky shiver drifted contentedly through her body. She responded by pressing into his caress, making tentative overtures of enjoyment. She returned the searching thrusts of his tongue and wondered how she could behave so unguardedly. But as he nuzzled a moist path along her cheek, caution seemed a petty intrusion. The sensations alternately racing and floating through her were too delicious to analyze. So she simply savored his scent and the quiet rhythm of his breathing. The rise and fall of his chest beneath her breasts created an unbearable tension inside her.

"Kylie." He reached her ear and circled its outline with his tongue before searching out the sensitive recesses within. Her fingers entwined the thickness of his dark hair as she tried to answer his whisper.

"Nick?" It was all she could manage over the slow rise of longing in her throat.

"Nothing. Just Kylie." He moved to the hollow below her ear, and then, deftly, smoothly, he turned her onto her back and positioned himself beside her. His lips found the pulsing ache in her throat and delivered a sensuous promise.

Deep in her mind Kylie heard the voices of reason whisper a warning. She meant to heed their counsel, but her fingers discovered the ripple of muscles across his back, and she had to explore further. *Another minute,* she soothed the voices. *Just another minute—or two.*

But the minutes slipped into timeless wonder as Nick returned to taste the sweetness of her mouth. Smoldering tension unfolded inside her with unsettling swiftness, and she forgot everything except the need to cling to him.

94

Forgot, that is, until she felt the edge of the game board pressing into her back.

She tried to shift away but couldn't seem to escape the sharp edge. "Nick," she murmured against his lips. "Nick, the—the Scrabble board. It's hurting me—"

He lifted her easily and shoved the intruder across the floor. The sound of the tiles scattering in confusion echoed the splintering of her control. Kylie knew she had to stop the seduction now or she wouldn't have the strength to stop it at all.

She felt the neckline of her blouse part at the insistence of his agile fingers and raised her hand to stop him. But Nick seemed to realize that it was only a token resistance, lacking any real conviction. His hand lowered to the next button, and her hand followed, not assisting but not getting in the way either. She felt the material separate to form a vee, felt the brush of his knuckles between her breasts, felt suddenly hot and breathless and languid.

Nick pressed a treacherously soft kiss on the exposed hollow before lifting his head and looking into her eyes. Once captured, she couldn't look away as he propped himself up on an elbow and rested his cheek on his palm. His other hand didn't rest, though. The scalloped edge of her bra burned against her skin with each foray of his fingers underneath it.

Thoughts trembled inside her. Questions. Answers. Scraps of reason that didn't seem reasonable at all. She had never experienced anything like this. Nick was different, and for the first time in a very long time she didn't want to be in control. She wanted to lose herself in his arms, to open herself to this new realm of feelings. But . . .

His tender smile quieted her uncertainty. Only the duskiness of his eyes revealed the depth of his emotion.

"Why do I get the feeling you're about to ask for a rain check, Kylie?"

She drew in her breath. "Would you—give me one?"

He skimmed a kiss from the corner of her mouth. "Only if you insist, and you're not going to do that."

"I'm not?" Was that shaky voice really hers?

"You don't stand a chance, you know. I've been taking assertiveness training."

She tried to frown away his confidence, but her lips lacked the desire to cooperate. The mere huskiness of his voice was magic. "It—it doesn't work with—things like this."

"Oh, I see. I'll have to mention that to my tutor—*later.*"

"Much later," she agreed and then felt the warmth of embarrassment, on her cheeks and in other, more vulnerable places. Uncertainty furrowed her brow. "I'm not sure I meant to say that."

His fingers trailed upward across her shoulders and neck to tangle in her hair, and his gaze followed. Over and over he brushed through the tendrils, seemingly mesmerized by the way they curled around his hand.

Kylie watched the cleft in his chin come and go, sensing and understanding his tension. Her palm curved along his jaw. "Nick?"

Slowly he turned his head the bare inch needed for him to meet her eyes. The laughter, the teasing was gone. In its place she saw a longing so intense that it spiraled inside her with echoing awareness.

"I'm rushing you, Kylie," he said in a throaty voice. "And I didn't intend to. I meant to give you plenty of time. Plenty of time." Almost against his will, it seemed, his hand moved to her shoulder and slipped the strap of her bra down her arm. Her blouse gave in to the downward slope, and Kylie made no move to stop it. With a gentle touch Nick lifted the lace covering her breast and lowered it to reveal the swelling fullness growing taut beneath his gaze. His finger circled the evidence of her desire as he searched her eyes for approval or denial. "I want to make love to you, Kylie."

Yes, her heart answered without hesitation, against all logic, against all reason. In her midnight dreams he was already her lover, seducing her with whispered promises and ethereal caresses. In her daydreams he was the seducer of her thoughts, the temptation she couldn't seem to resist. And she couldn't resist him now.

"Nick." His name was no more than a sliver of sound, but it seemed to echo in the quiet room. Shadows of doubt clouded his eyes as he watched her, and she knew somehow that he thought she was going to refuse.

"Nick, I—"

"Shhh." His hand went to her lips, urging silence. "I know it's too soon for you. It's all right. Waiting will only make the loving sweeter."

"Waiting?"

He drew back as if he couldn't bear to be so close and not be allowed to touch her. "I haven't changed my mind, Kylie. We will be lovers. Not tonight, but soon."

She lifted her hands to his shoulders, preventing him from moving farther from her side. "Assertiveness principle number four, Nick—don't procrastinate."

"What?"

Invitation tipped her smile. "I said, Never put off until tomorrow what you can do—tonight."

Her meaning registered in the tension-filled stillness that settled over him. His gaze touched her eyes, her lips, her breast in soft desire. Then he bent his head and possessed her mouth with tender reverence. His lips trembled slightly, betraying a depth of feeling that quickened her pulse and tightened her arms in an encircling embrace.

Kylie threaded her fingers through his hair, exerting just enough pressure to deepen the kiss. She dared to tease him with her tongue, content with tentative explorations while his breath filled her.

Their lips clung, parted, then met again. Passion skimmed her veins, robbing her of the last vestige of contentment and leaving her unbearably warm. Now her mouth opened eagerly to accept the imperative demands of his tongue. She had imagined this experience so many times, imagined the powerful seduction of his possessive embrace. But she had never imagined anything that came close to the yearnings that burned inside her. Desire stirred in the pit of her stomach, and her body arched against him in ardent communication.

Smoothly, without breaking the contact of the kiss, Nick sat up, pulling her with him. Then, one agonizingly slow button at a time, he finished unbuttoning her blouse and eased it from her. His lips traced a gentle path over her cheek to the sensitive spot below her ear. Kylie let her head fall against her shoulder to give him access to the curves and hollows of her neck.

Nick discovered each one with tantalizing deliberation as he loosened the fastener of her bra and freed her breasts. She felt wonderfully free and desirable as he leaned back to view her unconcealed beauty. Until that moment Kylie had never found beauty in her body, but now the look in his eyes told her it was there.

With hands that shook she reached toward him, obsessed with the need to see and touch him. He helped her pull the knit shirt up and over his head. Kylie tossed it aside and stared at the dark hair on his chest that invited her exploration. Her fingertips slid lightly through the crisp texture as Nick bent to take the tip of her breast into his mouth. Shivers coursed beneath the surface of her skin as he alternately teased and sucked her nipple. There seemed to be a soft melodic rhythm in the air, and gradually she realized it was the blending of their heartbeats. A melody so hypnotic that she lost all sense of time and movement in its song.

Kylie was dreamily aware that there was too much empty space around her, too much air cooling her. She cupped Nick's face in her hands, letting her thumbs stroke the corners of his mouth as he kissed her flesh. Her eyes closed in sensual delight as he slowly pulled away from her breast and began to nip at the fleshy pad of her thumb. With a gentle nudge she persuaded him to lift his head and give her room to nestle into his warmth.

Enclosed in the cloak of his embrace, she tried to savor the myriad sensations racing through her. But his every movement brought some new awareness of him, turning the heat of desire to sublimated fire.

Against her breasts Kylie felt the sigh that rose in his chest with erotic roughness. Like rubbing against the nap of velvet. Rich and stimulating and infinitely pleasurable.

Nick rediscovered the taste of her lips as his hand glided beneath the back waistline of her jeans. The snug denim refused to give and trapped his palm against her hips. Kylie released the snap and zipper and moaned softly as he pressed her backward into the carpet. His fingers splayed across the heated skin of her stomach, slipped inside her bikini panties, and found the secrets of her femininity.

On some vague plane of awareness Kylie felt him strip away her jeans, knew she assisted in their removal. She knew also that she watched him shrug free of his clothes and caressed his body with her gaze. But the momentary separation seemed a superfluous interruption of their intimacy. She wanted Nick beside her, around her, and in her, and anticipation fueled the flames of her yearning.

He knelt beside her and lightly, tenderly stroked her.

He investigated the supple length of her legs, beginning with fingertip circles of her ankles and moving steadily along her calves. Lingering over the slim curve of her thigh, he paused to trace, then kiss, the tiny birthmark there.

As he straightened to continue his exploration, Kylie thought she would melt in the silvery admiration of his eyes. Without haste he sculpted the contours of her stomach and hips and spanned her waist with gentle fingers.

Her breath caught as he took the weight of her breasts, cupping and molding his hands to conform to her curves. Still he wasn't satisfied and renewed the stroking caresses across her shoulders and throat until at last he framed her face in his hands. Slowly he bent to take her mouth in a fleeting promise.

It seemed an eternity before his body blanketed her, before his lips branded her soul. And then eternity became meaningless as she was consumed by the union of their flesh.

All the torrid colors of a summer sunset blurred in her mind, and she whirled through their fiery center. She felt the searing heat of their brilliance, reveled in the radiance surrounding her, and held fast to Nick, the essence of the night.

They reached a wild explosion of sensation and then ebbed into languorous emotion. Cradled at Nick's side, Kylie drifted into the soothing aftermath. The sound of his breathing lulled her, but reality intruded with the muffled chime of the grandfather clock. Eleven o'clock. Time for good-nights and separate bedrooms.

Nick tightened his arm around her and breathed a contented sigh. Kylie echoed the breathy vibration, knowing their nightly routine was altered irrevocably, just as everything between them was altered. For better or worse there could be no going back.

She wouldn't even if she could. How could she possibly feel any regret for what had just happened? Perhaps foolishly she had allowed her impulsive heart to rule her head. Perhaps she should have given more consideration to the arguments her logic had offered. She could think of a thousand perhapses, but not one of them would dull the quiet feeling of discovery inside.

The storm of passion had swept aside her illusions and given her a glimpse of deep emotion. She was special to Nick, just as he was special to her in some intangible, inexplicable way. Tonight she had taken a risk, made a conscious decision, and there could be no regrets.

His breath fanned her cheek, and Kylie closed her eyes in exquisite wonder. Lovers. She'd never known it could be so good. As she lifted her lips to invite his kiss she wondered if there had ever really been a decision to make.

CHAPTER SIX

It was the smile. Definitely the smile. Kylie leaned closer to her reflection in the mirrored tiles beside the tub. Above a cloud of iridescent bubbles the woman who looked back at her smiled. Serenely. Sensuously. Smugly.

Yes, Kylie decided. It was definitely the smile that betrayed her. She might have been able to ignore the mysterious sparkle in her eyes. And surely the softly persistent hint of blush in her cheeks wouldn't be noticed by anyone else. But it was hard to explain away that smile.

Not that anyone had asked. Not once during the entire day had anyone asked. She had received compliments on her dress, her hairstyle, even on the shade of lipstick she wore. Each *thank you* she'd murmured in response had been chaperoned by a stern command to the silent laughter inside her. She had wanted to laugh aloud with the knowledge that her dress wasn't new, her hairstyle was the same as the day before, and her lipstick was no more than a tinted gloss.

She was different because of Nick, because of the night

spent in his arms. And the difference showed in the satisfied curve of her mouth.

She had drifted through the day like Cinderella at the ball—composed on the surface, tremulously excited beneath. No one could have faulted her morning lecture on self-discipline. No one could have known the self-discipline it required to keep her smile under control whenever she looked toward the corner of the room. And she'd looked often for the reassurance of his presence, for the gentle encouragement in his eyes. She had glanced at Nick, glanced away, and returned to share a secret look, sweetened with a lover's promise.

Kylie lifted a wet fingertip to the mirror and tried to erase the smile, but it left her lips only to dance audaciously in her eyes. Wrinkling her nose at the image, she turned and sank up to her chin in the bath. It was warm and deliciously cozy, and even though she knew she shouldn't, Kylie couldn't resist lingering a moment longer. She was tempted to call to Nick and invite him to join her, but he was probably already dressed and waiting for her.

The thought of persuading him to skip Glynnis Claybrook's party in favor of an intimate evening for two was enticing. But she had promised Stephanie. Well, she hadn't actually promised because Stephanie hadn't actually voiced a plea for support.

"Are you going to be at the party tonight?" Stephanie had asked. But Kylie had recognized the entreaty in the blue eyes and she hadn't imagined the relief that edged Stephanie's smile at Kylie's affirmative answer.

Still, if Nick had shown even the slightest inclination to skip the party, Kylie knew she would happily have forgotten about Stephanie, Alex, Glynnis Claybrook, and the world at large. But Nick had seemed content with the plans for the evening. After work he'd taken her to a restaurant for dinner. When they returned to the house, he'd kissed her and whispered that she had just under an hour to get ready for the party.

And she had spent almost that amount of time lazing in the tub. She moved one leg, sliding it across the bathtub's porcelain bottom before raising her foot up out of the water. With toes pointed toward the ceiling Kylie watched the soap bubbles glide over her calf to splash into the bath.

Get out of the tub, she told herself sternly. *The water is getting cold, and it's getting late. Get out and get ready before Nick comes looking for you.*

At the thought her smile returned in full measure. That was exactly what she was hoping for, of course. If Nick should find her like this, he wouldn't remember the plans he'd made for the evening. She'd make sure of it.

With a determined sigh she sat upright, flipped the lever to open the drain, and forced herself to stand and step out onto the mat. As she rubbed her body briskly with the bath towel, Kylie decided she must stop acting as if the next few hours were all she had to spend alone with Nick. There would be hours after the party, all day tomorrow, the entire weekend, in fact. She still had another week and a half in Santa Fe and after that—

Her thoughts ran smack into a brick wall at that point, and Kylie flung the towel over the railing to dry and walked into her bedroom. All day she had successfully avoided facing the questions that followed words like *after that.* She didn't want to consider the future. Not now, anyway.

She wouldn't spoil this time of getting acquainted, this time of relaxing and enjoying every aspect of her new relationship with Nick. A discussion of the future would just complicate things right now. It would make demands that neither of them was ready to face. It was better to let these things develop naturally at their own pace.

There, Kylie thought as she pulled on her panty hose

and a camisole top. That made perfect sense. You couldn't rush emotions. It was better to take one day at a time and not make pointless speculations about the future. Perfectly logical reasoning, she congratulated herself. Positive thinking would achieve positive results.

But as the soft fabric of her dress slipped over her head and nestled around her in a smooth fit, her optimistic attitude faded. It was all perfect nonsense, she admitted. She wanted desperately to ask Nick how he felt about the future in general and a future with her in particular. But it was too soon for that, too soon to consider any kind of permanent arrangement.

So why did her thoughts keep coming back to words like *commitment* and *permanent?* Kylie whirled slowly to view her full-length reflection in the mirror. From the stocking-clad feet to the upswept cluster of curls crowning her head, she looked poised and composed. The dress was a misty blue complement to her femininity. Kylie smiled. Serenely, sensuously, smugly. Her thoughts kept coming back to words like *commitment* and *permanent* because she believed in happy endings. Even if it was too soon to think about any kind of ending at all.

A quiet tap on the door brought her pivoting gracefully, eagerly in that direction. Nick pushed open the door and stepped inside, his expression exactly matching the happy feelings bubbling inside her. He was dressed in dark pants; he was without a jacket, and the ends of his tie hung loosely from his white shirt collar.

Her fingers ached with the longing to dishevel his dusky hair and touch the roguish slant of his lips. "Hi," she said, her breath tumbling past the word to make it a whispery sigh.

"Hi," he answered in the same bemused manner, as if they hadn't parted company only minutes before.

"I guess I'm going to make us late," she offered questioningly.

"I'd say that's a pretty safe bet." He swept a long appreciative glance over her. "I came to see if you needed any help."

"Getting dressed, you mean?" Kylie taunted. "Somehow, I don't think you'd be much help in that department."

"I'll admit it goes against my natural instincts, but I've always been intrigued by the scenes in old movies where the heroine needs some assistance with a hook and eye or a zipper or something. I've always thought it would be nice to have a woman fasten my cuff links or straighten my tie." Nick lifted one wrist and pointed to the button fastening of his cuff with disdain. "But times have changed, and I don't wear cuff links."

Kylie shook her head in sympathy. "And I'm hopeless when it comes to men's ties."

"Maybe I could finish zipping your dress," he suggested hopefully.

"Unfortunately this dress doesn't have a zipper." She made a slow turn to demonstrate.

"So I see," he said with a frown. "Progress! Who needs it? No cuff links. No zippers. It's getting damned hard to find an excuse for being late these days."

Kylie stood, silently waiting, her senses absorbed in savoring his presence.

"Such a shame too." Nick crossed the room and stopped in front of her. He lifted a finger to stroke her cheek. "Especially since I've already phoned to say we'll be late arriving."

"Mmmm. That *is* a shame." She slid her palms over his silken shirt front and idly unbuttoned the top button. "I suppose I could change into a dress with a zipper."

106

"That seems like a terrible waste of time and energy. I can think of much better things to do."

"Such as?"

He smiled slowly and seductively as he bent his head to demonstrate his meaning. Kylie parted her lips to accept his kiss. The anticipation that trembled within her brought her up on tiptoe and into his arms.

Her hands followed the curve of his shoulders to caress his muscled back. His touch was gentle and deep, unhurried and yet full of urgency. She pressed against him, the clefts and angles of her body seeking and finding his corresponding symmetry. Entwined in his embrace, she discovered new delights, new sensations, which rippled through her like an incoming tide.

Kylie marveled at the pleasure that arced between them, at the almost unbelievable sense of belonging she felt. She wondered if Nick felt the same, if he experienced the same awareness of blending emotions, melding desires. It was the special quality that had drawn them inexorably together and now bound them in the tenuous threads of passion. And judging by her heated response, the threads seemed destined to forge a web of interwoven strengths.

At the gentle prompting of his tongue she opened her mouth to receive him. She welcomed the exploration and wanted to invite more. She felt her body sigh in surrender and knew she would never get enough of his touch.

In a smooth line from her neck to her waist to her hip, Nick's hands glided down her back. He drew her closer with tantalizing strokes. His knuckles brushed the outer swell of her breast and then retreated to the indentation of her waist. Reluctantly, lingeringly he broke the contact of their lips and traced a pathway of warm kisses to her earlobe.

"If this thing doesn't have a zipper," he whispered huskily, "how do I get you out of it?"

107

With a soft laugh Kylie stepped from the circle of his arms and slipped the dress up and over her head as easily as she had slipped it on only moments before. Her hands moved to the hem of the camisole, but Nick stopped her, obviously intent on removing it himself. Kylie looked into his eyes with a teasing smile. "It doesn't have a zipper either."

"I think I can manage," he said and proceeded to prove that he could. His gaze caressed her slowly, sending a thundering wave of longing through her. She reached for the dangling ends of his tie and tugged him closer. Her fingers trembled a little as she unbuttoned his shirt.

His hands rested like warm patches low on either side of her waist, and his chest rose and fell beneath the brush of her fingertips. Kylie thought he must surely hear the quickening rhythm of her heartbeat. With delicious curiosity she placed her palm flat against him and listened with her body to the sound of his matching rhythm.

Lifting her chin, she looked into his eyes, sharing the wonder of two hearts beating a duplicate pattern of desire. Nick responded by pressing his hand above her breast before he lowered it to cover the firm silky flesh.

A slow, intoxicating weakness filtered through her, and she stepped back, clutching the ends of his tie once more to pull him with her. Just as she felt the edge of the bed against her knees, he gave her a gentle push, and she toppled onto the coverlet.

His tie came with her, but Nick remained standing at the foot of the bed, half-dressed and looking down at her with a slumberous, expectant gaze. She returned his look with an encouraging tilt of her head, and then, in wanton anticipation, she gripped the waistband of her pantyhose and wiggled free of the sheer covering.

At the sound of his deep, indrawn breath a sudden unaccountable shyness came over her, and Kylie wanted to pull the coverlet around her nakedness. But instead she lifted her hand to him.

Nick reached out to cup her fingers in his. His touch was strong, reassuring, and tender. Infinitely tender. As if he understood, better than she, the emotions that flamed within her and betrayed her into eagerness. Then he undressed, leaving his shirt and slacks to gather wrinkles on the floor, lowered himself onto the bed, and gathered Kylie into his arms.

Her moan of pleasure was quickly smothered by the scorching possession of his kiss, which went on and on. He intensified the pressure, then drew back to tease and tantalize her mouth before once again deepening the caress. Her desire sparked and burned hotter as Nick led her skillfully into the fire. His hands were emissaries of passion, burning her with sensuous mastery. Kylie interpreted their message and communicated her own rising need with long discovering strokes of his body.

Fevered shivers of pleasure followed one another down her back as he moved her beneath him and began to satisfy the ache he had created. It was a gentle, leisurely fulfillment that built to an impassioned climax, then ebbed into a beautifully complete satisfaction. Pliant and yielding, Kylie feathered her fingers through the silken wetness of his chest, wanting nothing more than to stay curled against his warmth for the rest of the night.

Nick rubbed her shoulder in sleepy circles, as if he were reluctant to leave the cozy nest of her arms. "I think we'll be fashionably late in arriving at the party now," he said with a trace of regret.

"I don't know," Kylie murmured in protest. "Maybe we should procrastinate a little longer."

His low chuckle vibrated beneath her hand. "Any longer and we'll arrive with the sunrise—if we arrive at all."

With a nod she sighed and pushed determinedly out of

his hold. "All right, then. We'd better get dressed—again." As she slid from the bed and began to look for her clothing, Kylie glanced back at him over her shoulder. "Honestly, Nick. Why didn't you think of this before I got dressed the first time?"

"Oh, I thought about it." He raised himself on an elbow to grin at her. "But you see, I heard this lecture today on self-discipline, and I was trying to—"

"Practice what I preach?"

"In a manner of speaking. Actually I was trying to find the flaw in your theory."

She sent him a sweet smile. "Well, you obviously found it. Otherwise we'd be at the party already, wouldn't we?"

"Would we, Kylie? I didn't notice any awesome display of self-discipline on your part, either."

"That's different. I was merely practicing some positive thinking." She walked around the bed to the bathroom door, ever-conscious of his appreciative regard.

"Positive thinking?" he asked, stopping her exit from the room.

She turned and lifted her shoulders in a provocative shrug. "I was thinking that it was *positively* ridiculous to go to a party when we had so many *better* things to do."

The curve of his lips held her captivated as he swung his feet to the floor and stood, a virile, enticing example of masculinity. "Better *things*?" The arch of his eyebrow was a teasing challenge. "You mean there's more?"

"That's for me to know and you to find out—later." She stepped into the bathroom and closed the door behind her.

"You bet I will, Kylie. You can count on it." The amused confidence of his voice carried clearly to her ears as she leaned against the door and let the smile that threatened have control.

"I am, Nick," she whispered in a voice too low for him to hear, and yet Kylie knew that somehow he had heard.

110

* * *

The party was at full tempo when Kylie and Nick slipped almost unnoticed into the crowd. It was a lively gathering with some forty or more guests dressed in everything from denims to diamonds. The noise level was somewhere between subdued and deafening, although it tended toward the latter. The food was good, the conversation varied, and the atmosphere quaint. A wandering guitarist strolled through the crowd, serenading anyone who glanced in his direction.

Kylie was impressed by the dark, Spanish beauty of Glynnis Claybrook and by the warmth of her welcome. But Kylie was less than impressed by the way Nick introduced her, first to her hostess and then to other guests. It wasn't what he said so much as what he didn't say. Not once did he mention the reason for her presence in Santa Fe.

It was an oversight on his part, she knew. Purely unintentional, but bothersome just the same. She could have mentioned the seminar, of course, quite naturally, and she felt sure Nick would have taken the cue. But for some perverse reason it seemed important that he recognize the omission on his own.

She told herself it was silly to be upset over something as trifling as an introduction, but she knew it went deeper than that. Nick saw her as a woman, first and last, and her profession had little or no significance for him. It was the way Colin had seen her, too, and she had allowed him to treat her accordingly. But she wouldn't allow it now, not from Nick.

"Kylie?"

With relief she turned from her disturbing thoughts to the woman behind her. From her softly curling hair to her softly curving smile, Stephanie looked light-years removed from the efficient, tailored, and cuffed Bunny.

Her vivid red gown began with off-the-shoulder ruffles that tucked neatly into a slender waist and flared in romantic tiers to the floor. "Stephanie," Kylie said warmly, "I've been wondering where you were."

"Alex has been showing me the garden."

It was a shy admission, almost reluctantly made, and it gave Kylie pause. That Alex had changed his attitude so abruptly was hard to believe, but the gentle blush on Stephanie's cheeks was evidence that something had changed. "And have you been showing Alex that brunettes can be far more fascinating than blondes?"

The blush deepened, but the blue eyes sparkled with pleasure. "I don't know about fascinating, Kylie, but he's talking to me. Really talking. And he hasn't mentioned the office more than once or twice." She stopped, and when she continued, her voice had lost some of its enthusiasm. "Well, maybe he's mentioned it three or four times, but still . . . it's a start, don't you think?"

Kylie smiled her encouragement, wondering privately how Alex inspired such affection. "Where is Alex, by the way?"

"He's getting me a drink." Stephanie nodded toward the bar where Alex stood chatting with Nick. "I'm in love with him, you know." Her blue eyes met Kylie's brown ones, then looked away. "I have been for a long time, but I never thought there was a chance . . ."

Kylie shifted uncomfortably, cautious about getting into a discussion of Stephanie's chances with Alex. With a guilty feeling of relief she noticed Nick turn and start toward her.

"I didn't think," Stephanie continued, "that Alex would ever see me as a woman and not as a secretary. Until your seminar, Kylie, I didn't realize that he saw me exactly the way I saw myself. I've been too efficient in the office, too willing to take on responsibilities that weren't

112

mine. There are going to be some changes in the executive suite, and Alex may not like them. But I'm not going to be afraid to stand up for myself, either in or out of the office. It may take a long time, but one way or another I'll earn his respect."

"More important, though, Stephanie, you're learning to respect yourself, to appreciate your own worth."

"Thanks to you."

Kylie shook her head in denial. "No. Motivation comes from within. You deserve the credit, not me."

"But I couldn't have done it without you."

"Secrets?" Nick asked as he handed Kylie a glass and smiled disarmingly at Stephanie. "Are you two plotting to liven up this party?"

"Of course," Kylie answered. "We were just waiting for you to join us."

"Breathlessly, I hope."

"Absolutely limp with anticipation." Stephanie colored but managed to meet Nick's amused look.

"Ah," he said wickedly. "At last, a woman who appreciates my charisma. You're a woman after my heart, Stephanie."

"All right, Cousin." Alex joined the conversation to complete the foursome. "You can quit flirting with my secretary now." He slipped a proprietary arm around Stephanie's bare shoulders. "The next thing I know, you'll be trying to steal Bunny and advance her up the corporate ladder to the home office."

Stephanie stiffened at his touch. Her eyes darkened in disappointment and then brightened with determination. Unobtrusively she moved free of Alex's hold. "If there's ever an opening in the home office, Mr. Braden, you wouldn't have to *steal* me. Just ask. I think I might like to live in San Francisco."

"Oh, come on, Bunny. You wouldn't leave Southwest

and me. We need you." Alex assumed his best soothing manner, but Stephanie responded with a cool stare.

"I need a drink, Alex. Did you forget?" With enviable control Stephanie spun away from any excuse that he might offer and walked toward the bar.

"I'll be damned!" Alex muttered as he watched the swirl of red skirt that marked her path. "What's wrong with her now?" He turned to Kylie in accusation. "What did you say to her? We were getting along fine until she started talking to you. I suppose I'll have to apologize now."

"Why don't you try a couple of dozen roses?" Kylie suggested with biting humor.

"Roses?" His blond brows soared in surprise. "For Bunny? You must be joking."

"Her name is Stephanie," Kylie said crisply, but to no avail. Alex had turned his back and was hurrying across the room. Pressing her lips together angrily, Kylie glanced at Nick and caught the glint of amusement in his eyes. "You could have said something, you know."

"Oh, no. I'm not getting involved in this little triangle. It's strictly none of my business . . . until it affects my business, if you understand what I mean." He sipped his drink, cool, unconcerned, and opinionated.

"I understand completely." She kept her voice low to conceal the twinge of irritation she felt at his attitude. "You'll allow, will even be entertained by, these minor skirmishes between two of your employees, but the instant they pose a threat to you personally—"

"Hey, what is this?" Nick interrupted with a questioning frown. "I'm just a bystander in all this. Alex and Stephanie can skirmish all they want outside of the office. Although it amazes me that any man could clash with such a potent combination of innocent blue eyes and that Scarlett O'Hara dress."

It was such a typically male comment that Kylie focused on it as the final straw to all the evening's minor irritations. "That's a very chauvinistic remark."

"Why?"

"Because it just is." She drew a deep breath. "You could have noticed something more important about Stephanie tonight. Like the confident way she's been speaking to people—to you, to Alex. That's the difference, you know. She's finally gained some self-confidence." Kylie flashed him a challenging glance. "You might at least admit some grudging admiration of her spirit."

"I admire her spirit," Nick said, lifting his drink in mock salute. "And I also admire her very . . . attractive dress."

"Men!" she murmured under her breath. "They're all alike."

His gray eyes laughed at her above the rim of his glass. "Careful," he admonished solemnly. "Someone might accuse you of making a chauvinistic remark."

A smile tugged at her lips, but she resisted stoically. "Excuse me," she said with a tilt of her chin. "I'm going to find a conversational partner who can look past a woman's clothing to the person beneath."

Kylie winced at her poor choice of words, but Nick merely arched his brows and wisely didn't follow through on the comment.

"Why don't you do that?" he answered in a maddeningly patient voice. "I'll find you when it's time to leave."

With a nod she moved to the opposite side of the room, wondering with each step why she was upset with Nick. Maybe things were moving too fast for her. Her gaze retraced her path to linger on his profile. How had his opinion and his attitudes become so important to her in such a short time?

Noticing her pensive study of him, Nick smiled, and

Kylie knew it was an open invitation to "agree to disagree." The sensible thing to do, of course. But she wouldn't return to his side, not just yet.

Kylie dulled the temptation with a second glass of wine and an intriguing conversation with a man she'd met earlier in the evening. Quite by chance she discovered he was a business owner from Albuquerque and that he was looking for an employee-incentive program.

She explained her own ideas and the basic premise of her seminars. He seemed receptive, even asked her to call him in a few weeks when she'd finished the training at Southwest. It sounded like a good opportunity, and she smiled easily at Nick when he touched her arm.

"Are you ready to leave?" he asked.

Kylie nodded. "I'll be in touch, Mr. Sanders."

The balding man looked past her to Nick. "Miss Richards has been telling me about her seminars. I was surprised to hear she's giving one for your company. You don't usually go in for that type of employee training, do you, Braden?"

"No." Nick put his hand at the small of Kylie's back and started to move away, but Mr. Sanders followed.

"But you did this time," the man persisted.

"Yes."

Kylie glanced at Nick in surprise, wondering at his terse answer.

"Miss Richards must have a seminar that's worthwhile, then," Mr. Sanders continued, obviously determined to get an answer out of Nick. "Do you recommend it, Braden?"

Kylie felt the tension that rippled through Nick as he reluctantly slowed his pace. His hand moved protectively to her shoulder and then down her arm in short soothing strokes as he faced Jonathan Sanders. Nick drew a deep breath but still hesitated before answering—just a second

116

or two, but long enough. "Miss Richards is very . . . capable."

The word stole through Kylie, leaving her shaken and disbelieving. *Capable?* It was worse than saying nothing at all. *Capable!* She wanted to vent some of her capabilities on Nick at that moment, but she kept a tight rein on her emotions. Somehow she managed a reassuring smile at Mr. Sanders. "I'll give you a call."

The man's gaze fell to where Nick's hand caressed her bare arm, soothingly, possessively, suggestively. Then he looked uncomfortably away, obviously drawing his own conclusions. "That's all right, Miss Richards. It would be best if I got in touch with you."

Kylie didn't remember saying good night to her hostess, and she didn't remember the walk to the car. But the drive home was something she knew she'd never forget. It was the coldest she'd ever had on a summer night. The silence was ear-splitting, but she would have died rather than say one word to Nick.

"I'm sorry, Kylie," Nick said the moment they entered the house. "I know you're upset, but I couldn't lie to the man."

She whirled on him. "No, of course you couldn't! And of course you couldn't say anything positive. You had to be honest. *Honest!* That's a laugh. *She's capable,* you said. And you stood there rubbing my arm like I was capable of . . . of . . . Do you realize what he thought, Nick? What you *let* him think?"

"I'm not responsible for what the man thought, Kylie. You know I had no intention of—"

"Of making such a . . . a dishonest insinuation?"

The cleft in his chin marked his irritation. "I've already apologized. If it will make you feel better, I'll call Sanders and explain the whole misunderstanding."

"No, thanks. I don't need your help. After I've finished

the seminar at Southwest, the production report will be all the explanation I need. Mr. Sanders will understand then . . . without any clarification from you."

"You haven't finished the seminar yet, Kylie."

His lack of confidence in her spurred her determination. "Oh, but I will, if only to prove to you how very *capable* I am. I hope you like crow, Nick, because you're going to eat your words, one by one, and I'm going to make sure you do."

He smiled, but his eyes, at last, held no hint of amusement. "I admire your spirit, Kylie. If that day ever comes, borrow Stephanie's dress, would you? I prefer to have dinner with a woman who at least looks feminine."

"And I prefer not to speak to a man who is so threatened by a woman's profession!" Kylie spun away from him, anger trembling inside her.

"Kylie, wait! Let me—"

"Save it for the Male Chauvinists' Club," she tossed over her shoulder. "I'm sure they'll appreciate your sentiments." Before he could respond, she controlled the impulse to flounce from the room and managed to make a dignified exit. She shoved the bedroom door closed behind her and took vengeful pleasure in the loud slam.

Taking off her dress and throwing it in a heap on the floor helped some. But as her initial anger wore away, Kylie knew nothing would help very much. She had no one to blame except herself. She'd known better than to get involved with Nick. She'd promised herself she wouldn't make that mistake. But she had. Blindly she had fallen for his smooth line, knowing all the time that there couldn't be a happy ending.

As she lay awake, feeling lonelier than she'd ever felt before, Kylie gave herself a stern lecture about being assertive and thinking positively. But somehow it only made her feel worse.

At least she wasn't in love with him, she thought sometime just before dawn. Well, all right, she admitted, maybe she was half in love with him. But only half, and if she looked on the bright side, that meant she only had to talk some sense into half of her heart. It was small comfort but the best she could manage under the circumstances. Half her heart, she thought, and wished desperately that she could smile.

CHAPTER SEVEN

Kylie discouraged a yawn by sipping at her coffee and focusing a disinterested gaze on the newspaper in her hand. The print blurred into a meaningless string of words, and finally she folded the paper and placed it on the sofa beside her. Restlessly she propped her feet on the coffee table and stared at the patio beyond the glass doors. The sun bathed the garden in morning light and streamed through the windows in warming streaks of gold. It was going to be a gorgeous day, full of blue sky and puffy clouds.

That was the trouble with the weather, Kylie thought. Just when you needed a drizzle of rain to match your mood, nature turned on the charm. Well, it would take more than a little sunshine to win a smile from her today.

Something from Nick, along the lines of an abject apology or a full-page mea culpa ad in *The New York Times,* might do the trick. Even the knowledge that he'd spent a sleepless night would have gone a long way toward dispelling her gloom. But he'd denied her even that small satisfaction.

He had, purposefully, she was sure, left his bedroom door open so she would know he wasn't bothered by their quarrel. At least not enough to let it keep him awake. He had been sleeping peacefully, like a grizzly bear in hibernation, when she'd walked past his door an hour ago. And from the lack of sound in his part of the house, she concluded he was probably still dreaming on.

But when he finally did awaken, he wouldn't find her staring dismally out the window. Kylie swung her feet to the floor in sudden decision. It was a beautiful morning, too beautiful to spend indoors. Santa Fe was a city steeped in rich history, and today she would be a tourist, a typical Polaroid-snapping tourist.

She would pack a lunch and visit any and every tourist attraction that caught her fancy. And sometime during the day she'd purchase a totally useless souvenir. Something a trifle gaudy perhaps, and emblazoned with the words *Souvenir of Santa Fe, New Mexico*. Something that in later years she'd shake her head over and wonder why she had wanted a reminder of a routine business trip.

In the kitchen Kylie made a sandwich, took an orange from the refrigerator, and rummaged through the cabinets for a paper sack. Once packed, it didn't seem like much of a lunch, and she wished she could work up a little more enthusiasm for her plans.

"Enthusiasm is a state of mind," she said aloud. "And state of mind is simply a matter of self-control." There was no immediate increase in the appeal of the lunch she'd made or in her outlook, and she closed the sack with a heavy sigh.

"I don't know who you have in there, but apparently they've heard that lecture before."

At the sound of Nick's voice her frown deepened. "I was talking to myself," she stated coolly.

"Well, it didn't seem to make much of an impression on you either."

Kylie dismissed his comments with an indifferent shrug and scolded the rebel cadence of her heart. Nick moved across her peripheral vision on his way to the refrigerator, and though she told herself not to, she turned to watch him. As he opened the door and bent to look inside, her gaze fell to the neat navy-blue running shoes on his feet and rose past the white sport socks with their navy trim to the tanned length of sinewy leg beneath the beige shorts. The navy-blue polo shirt was stretched over his shoulders, and Kylie mustered her defenses against the tremor of longing that threatened her composure.

"Hungry?" he asked, his voice muffled by the refrigerator.

"No!" It was too quick, too loud, and too defensive, and she made an effort to soften her tone. "No."

Nick straightened, the orange juice container in his hand, and let the door swing closed. He glanced in her direction, then warily looked away. "I guess I slept through breakfast."

"I guess you did." Kylie lifted the lunch sack and held it in front of her like a shield.

While he took a glass from the cabinet and filled it with juice, she stood quietly, wishing she could just walk from the kitchen and leave him to wonder about her plans. But it seemed crucial to the enjoyment of her day that Nick should know about and appreciate her total lack of concern for his breakfast, lunch, or afternoon snack. She didn't care what he did as long as he understood that she had no interest whatsoever in his plans. That her logic bordered on illogic only made her more determined to show him a totally feigned indifference.

"I'm leaving now," she announced.

His level gray eyes regarded the sack in her hands. "I thought perhaps you were running away from home."

"This isn't my home, and I'm not running away. I'm going sight-seeing."

He nodded and took a drink of his juice. "What sights are you going to see?"

"I don't know. What do you suggest?" Kylie frowned at her question. She hadn't intended to ask his opinion.

"I suggest you get a guide. Someone who knows the area and can take you behind the scenes." He lifted the glass to his lips once more. "Of course, it's difficult to find an experienced guide."

"I would think they'd be a dime a dozen."

"Oh, no. We're a small, select group."

"We?"

Nick arched one eyebrow in surprise. "Didn't I mention that?" He smiled with assumed modesty. "In my spare time I sometimes conduct tours of the area. Only for special VIPs, of course, and only on alternate Saturdays when it doesn't rain."

"What a pity." She shook her head in feigned disappointment. "I'm sure I just heard a distant rumble of thunder. Maybe some other—"

"All right," he interrupted with a lift of his hand. "I'll make an exception for you, Kylie. But you have to promise not to let word get around that I'm a soft touch."

"Don't worry, Nick. I would never breathe a word that might support such a nasty rumor. It's probably a good thing that I'm not asking you to join me."

"Would it help if I offered to negotiate the fee?" He eyed the sack in her hand hungrily. "I might consider—"

She clutched the sack closer to her. "Oh, no, you don't. This is my lunch. You'll have to make your own."

He shrugged his concession. "All right. I'll fix a lunch

123

and be ready to go in five minutes. Is that soon enough for you?"

"No! Yes. I mean—" She broke off the protest and tipped her chin. "I think I should spend the day by myself."

He moved to within inches of her defiant stance. "And I think we should spend the day together," he said and leaned even closer. "Would you care to settle this disagreement with the flip of a coin?"

His breath stirred warm shivers of memory in her, and she nervously moistened her lips. "There's no disagreement to settle."

"Good." His voice was suddenly husky, soft, and serious. "Because I want to be with you, Kylie."

She melted when she saw the tender request in his eyes. Her resistance ebbed in direct proportion to the upward slant of his mouth, and when the intriguing cleft appeared in his chin, she surrendered to the misguided insistence of her heart.

"Five minutes," she stated crisply, knowing that if he exhibited the tiniest glimmer of triumph, she would withdraw the invitation. Nick didn't attempt to conceal the relief that completed his smile as he stepped back and turned again to the refrigerator. Kylie watched him for a minute, taking a guilty delight in the knowledge that he wanted to spend the day with her. She should have stood firm in her resolve to act sensibly and stay as far away from him as possible, but her heart put up a strong argument. And she didn't seem to have much control over her emotions anymore.

With a wry frown Kylie walked from the kitchen. Who was she kidding? From the moment she'd met him, she had had precious little control over any part of her life. Why should today be any different?

In all honesty, though, she had to admit that Nick made

a concerted effort to consult her wishes during their leisurely tour of Santa Fe. With the expertise of an experienced guide and a patient half smile, he accompanied her through the fiestalike atmosphere of the central plaza.

The casual touch of his hand at the small of her back made Kylie achingly aware of him. Even amidst the crowd that strolled the block-long avenue of native vendors, she was conscious of Nick, of his deep voice, the latent amusement in his eyes, his elusive masculine scent. She was glad they weren't alone and in the same instant wished they were.

If he suspected her ambivalent feelings, Nick gave no indication of it. He was lighthearted, attentive, and witty and displayed a considerable knowledge of the history and culture of New Mexico and her people. And to his credit he showed no surprise at her rather curious choice of a souvenir when she bypassed the displays of turquoise and silver jewelry to purchase a cactus-shaped salt and pepper set.

Kylie snapped pictures with a reckless finger, trying to capture the old-world charm of adobe buildings, and succeeded in capturing Nick within the photographic lens more often than not.

When Nick insisted he would soon pass out from lack of nourishment if they didn't stop for lunch, Kylie was glad of an excuse to leave history behind. It was becoming difficult to concentrate on her surroundings, no matter how charming, with Nick so close by her side. With so much still to discover about him it seemed almost frivolous to spend any time discovering a city that had been around for centuries and would certainly be around for years to come.

The drive from Santa Fe into the national park to the east was accomplished in comfortable silence. It gave her time to take a deep breath, relax, and adjust to the change from noisy crowds to the quiet murmuring of nature—and time to study the easy way Nick drove and kept her fascinated by the simple movement of his hands.

The picnic spot he chose bordered a swift mountain stream that flowed musically past the stones in its path. The clear water and deep-green vegetation provided a colorful setting for the blanket Nick spread over the grass. Kylie eyed the blanket doubtfully before she sat cross-legged on one corner.

"A tablecloth?" she asked. "Are you always so well prepared?"

He placed her lunch sack in front of her and seated himself before opening his considerably larger sack. "Oh, this is just spur of the moment. If I'd had more time, we would have had a picnic to remember, complete with red-checkered cloth and woven basket."

"Packed with a wedge of cheese, a loaf of bread, and a jug of wine, no doubt." Kylie unwrapped her sandwich and nibbled at the crust.

Nick followed her example. "That certainly is poetic, but I think I prefer a picnic with more substance."

"I noticed."

"No snide remarks from your side of the blanket, please. You should keep it in mind that I have the only two cans of soda in the immediate vicinity."

"That is something to consider. Would you trade one can of soda for half of an orange?"

He reached inside his sack and withdrew the can, holding it for a minute before passing it to her. "There's something unfair about this transaction, but in the interest of my future as a tour guide, I won't quibble."

"Hmmm," Kylie murmured after taking a sip. "I had a feeling this would cost me. I suppose you expect my eternal gratitude."

"That wasn't exactly what I expected."

126

Kylie ignored the question inherent in the words and focused her attention on lunch.

"Well?" he asked finally. "Aren't you going to ask what I did expect?"

"No." Her lips formed an innocent curve. "In the interest of your future as a tour guide, I think it's best that I not know. I'm afraid it might lead to a personal and very *unprofessional* discussion."

Nick stretched out on the blanket, propping himself up on an elbow and lifting his brows in mock surprise. "I see you've been picnicking here before."

"Let's just say I recognize a line when I hear one."

He laughed with quiet enjoyment. "Where have you been all my life, Kylie?"

Waiting for you, her heart said so clearly she wondered that he didn't hear it. Her brown eyes met his gray ones, and for a moment she shared his smile. "I've been learning how to handle fresh tour guides who get out of hand."

"You can handle me any way you like." Nick grinned as he reached for a bag of chips. "It would be nice if you'd wait until I've finished lunch, but if you're anxious—?"

Kylie managed to keep from choking and took a drink of soda to restore her composure. "I'll restrain myself somehow."

"Just until I've finished lunch," he amended.

"Which by the look of it will be sometime tomorrow afternoon."

He glanced defensively at the remaining sandwich, bag of chips, pickle, and sack of cookies. "If I start now, I'm sure I'll be through in time to show you the sunrise. Maybe even a little nature by moonlight."

Images flooded her mind—of Nick, his face shadowed and tender in the light of a thousand stars, of trees bending to shelter a grassy bed, of the midnight sounds of a summer night, of the scent of mountains. It was all there in

127

her mind, so vivid she could almost feel the touch of his lips on hers.

"Of course," he said, his voice sending the images flying to the far corners of her dreams, "there is an extra charge for late-night tours."

With an effort Kylie imitated his teasing tone. "Let me guess—breakfast?" She shook her head. "I'm afraid my expense account will never stretch that far. You see, my employer isn't very open-minded."

Nick smiled at the sally, but she could tell he wasn't amused. Kylie turned her attention to the rest of her sandwich and wished she hadn't mentioned their business relationship. All day Nick had skillfully directed the conversation away from controversial subjects to ensure that the time they spent together was light and enjoyable.

And she had enjoyed every minute, every smile. It was pleasant to feel so relaxed with Nick, and she didn't want to spoil it.

Tossing the empty sandwich wrapper into the sack, Kylie shifted her position and then settled back to observe the rushing stream as she peeled the orange. She glanced at Nick and wondered what he was thinking behind his pensive expression.

Was he thinking of her? Imagining how she would look with moon dust glinting in her hair? Kissing her in his daydreams? Or were his thoughts distant and far removed from this idyll? Impulsively she broke the orange in half and leaned toward him, knowing it was a ploy to gain his attention again, knowing that she didn't want to share his thoughts with anything else at the moment.

"Here's your half," she teased coaxingly.

He swung his gaze to her outstretched hand as if he'd forgotten her presence. Then he shook his head. "No, thanks. I'm full."

Slowly she withdrew the proffered fruit. "And here I thought you had the appetite of a growing boy."

Nick lay back, cupping his hands behind his head and closing his eyes. "Boy," he repeated quietly. "I haven't been a boy since I was eight years old. Before my father died, he told me I was the man of the family, that I should take care of my mother."

"And you did," Kylie stated in a voice little more than a whisper.

"I didn't know there was a choice. At that age I took promises very seriously."

"Somehow I don't think age would have made any difference."

"Maybe not," he conceded. "Perhaps it's just that time teaches you how to avoid making promises you can't or don't want to keep."

Kylie tried to visualize Nick as a child, but the image slipped through her mind too quickly to take form. "Do you regret keeping that particular promise?"

"How can I answer that, Kylie? I don't regret it, but there are times when I wonder what it would have been like to grow up with little or no responsibility."

She nibbled on an orange section and mulled his words over in her mind. "I would have thought you had a dramatic example of irresponsibility in Alex."

Nick gave a soft chuckle. "If you ever met my Aunt Rosemary, you'd understand Alex's belief that the world was made expressly for him. I'm not making excuses for him. I think he should have cut the apron strings long ago. But my aunt can be very persuasive, and she'd never given him the opportunity to make a decision on his own."

"Until my seminar," Kylie added. She felt the caution in Nick's studied pause and pretended not to notice his hesitation. "You said yourself that Alex had to take full responsibility for that."

"Alex may have made the decision all on his own, Kylie, but you can be sure he was counting on his mother's support in case there were any repercussions."

"Which there were, as a matter of fact."

A soft breath left his lips. "I wouldn't touch that line for a two-week vacation in Tahiti."

With a fleeting smile Kylie shifted back to a safer subject. "What about Alex's father?"

"No one ever had the nerve to ask about him. It's possible that he left her. Few men could live with my aunt's dynamic energy level and fierce independence. You can see what happened to Alex."

"She sounds like quite a formidable person."

"She can be," Nick said. "But she is also one of the most charming women you could ever hope to meet. In fact, with the exception of my mother I can't think of another woman I admire more."

A ripple of wounded vanity wound through Kylie. It was foolish of her even to think that she might be the woman he most admired. Foolish and so typically female. She frowned at her own stupidity. "Does your mother work in the home office too?"

"My mother is content to let me look out for her interests in the corporation. She tells me she simply has no business sense, that men are better with financial reports and sales charts. Actually she just likes to have someone take care of the things that she feels are a man's responsibility. She needs someone to make life's mundane decisions for her so that she can concentrate on making life gracious."

Kylie let her gaze trace his profile with intuitive understanding. "And you're that someone, aren't you, Nick?"

"There wasn't anyone else for her to depend on until a year ago, when she remarried. He's a southern gentleman

130

who treats her like a fragile magnolia blossom, and she's blissfully happy these days."

"And are you blissfully happy these days too?"

Nick rolled onto his side and trapped her in his amused gaze. "Only on alternate Saturdays when it doesn't rain."

"It isn't raining today," she answered warily.

"No, it isn't, is it?" His lips curved, not with a smile but in caressing invitation. "Come here, Kylie."

A butterfly feeling danced wildly inside her, and she wanted nothing more than to obey him, yet she hesitated. "My hands are sticky, Nick. I've been eating an orange."

His gaze dropped to her hands, then backtracked to her lips. "I've always liked the taste of oranges."

Pushing herself to her feet, Kylie looked down at him. "I'll just wash the stickiness off and be right back," she announced as if her voice wasn't shaky and lacking in conviction. As she made her way to the stream's graveled bank, she wondered why she was so reluctant to give in to her own longing to be in his arms. Was it possible that she recognized the danger in each surrender, no matter how small? That she knew each soft word and gentle touch brought her closer to the time when she would be unable to reclaim even the tiniest section of her heart? The water swirled around her fingers in soothing ripples, and she admitted it was more than possible. She sensed Nick's presence behind her before she felt his hands on her shoulders. With a sigh she acknowledged her reprehensible feeling of relief that he had made the decision for her.

"Here, let me help," he said, bending beside her. His large hands captured hers beneath the surface and sent shivers of pleasure racing up her arms.

"That's all right, Nick. I can manage." She shifted her weight and lost her balance, leaning precariously over the stream.

"Watch out." He brought his hands up to catch her and

splashed water over them both. When she was settled back on her heels, Nick took his hands from her sides, leaving two wet patches on her T-shirt as a reminder of his help. "I thought you were just going to rinse off the stickiness," he said. "But if you're intent on a bath, I'll have to guide you to a more secluded spot."

Kylie arched an eyebrow at his teasing. Then she cupped some water in her palm and flipped it toward his face. "Anyone can lose their balance, Mr. Braden. Even you."

Nick blinked at the watery assault and retaliated in kind before she could defend herself. "It takes a very assertive push to knock me off balance, but if you care to give it a try, Miss Richards . . ."

Kylie laughed as she wiped the drops from her face. "I wouldn't want you to get all wet."

Taking her by the shoulders, Nick grinned wickedly. "Well, I would like very much for you to get all wet. Then you'd have to change into something more—comfortable, wouldn't you?"

Her eyes widened with suspicion. "Nick? You wouldn't *really*—"

He did, and Kylie found herself sitting half-in and half-out of the stream. The only consolation was that Nick lost his balance and got twice as wet as she did. She intended to give him her best disapproving scowl, but at the sound of his rich laughter her intention fled. His amusement was just too infectious to resist, and she joined him.

Then she was leaning toward him, offering her lips, wanting to taste the moistness that lingered on his mouth. As their lips met, Kylie knew it was a taste she would always associate with Nick. A kiss both tender and demanding, full of the gentle strength so characteristic of him.

Bringing her palms up to cup his face, she let her body

relax against him, let the kiss deepen as he shifted his weight to support her. Kylie gave in to the subtle pressure and felt desire swirl and eddy inside her.

The mountain stream might have been a tropical pool, lying warm and sultry beneath a blazing sun. The cool water flowing around her felt heated and enticing, and Kylie couldn't imagine a more sensuous feeling.

His hands slipped beneath her shirt, pushing her bra aside impatiently to reach the sensitive flesh beneath. Her breasts strained toward him, lifting and tightening in response to his touch. The dampness clinging to his palms heightened the sensation of his caress, adhering skin to skin and robbing her of the ability to breathe.

There was something timeless in a kiss shared amidst the elements. There was the blending of all the colors and fragrances in nature's palette to complement the blending of a man and a woman—a sense of oneness that transcended the senses to reach the soul. Deep within her Kylie knew this, was conscious of the awesome beauty of the mountains and trees, of the sky and swirling stream. And she knew also that all this was insignificant compared to the awesome yearning of her heart for this man.

When he drew back, her sigh was one of reproach. "Mmmm," she murmured. "Could we try that again? You see, no one has ever kissed me in the middle of a stream before, and I want to be sure I've got the hang of it."

"Sorry." Nick stood and pulled her up with him. "I can't divulge trade secrets. The next thing I know you'd be offering guided tours to this very spot."

Kylie wound her arms invitingly around his neck. "Do you suppose a little positive action on my part could change your mind?"

His fingers teased their way down her back to her hips. "Blackmail, Kylie?"

"Friendly persuasion, Nick." She applied pressure to

his nape and raised herself on tiptoe to brush his lips with hers. He was slow to respond, letting her make the initial overtures. With the tip of her tongue she explored the sensuous curve of his mouth and the tantalizing taste inside until he gave in to her allure and tightened his hold on her. Their bodies clung, wet and warm with the currents of desire that built to a demanding crest but halted at Nick's command.

"Kylie," he said in a throaty whisper, "has anyone ever made love to you in the middle of a stream?"

She shook her head and nestled against him. "I guess it might be a little uncomfortable."

"My thinking, exactly," he said firmly. "So let's leave the friendly persuasion until a more propitious moment, shall we?"

"Your wish is my command."

His eyes communicated his skepticism as he took her hand and led her from the water. "I'd better get you home. I think you're becoming delirious. Overexposure to nature, more than likely."

It was overexposure to Nick, Kylie thought as they packed the remnants of their lunch and started toward Santa Fe. *Too much of anything isn't good for you,* she remembered her mother saying. *You can't have too much of a good thing,* her father would always counter. Kylie glanced at Nick and decided that in this instance she liked her father's advice better.

Nick turned and caught her look, returning it with a smile. "You look very pleased with yourself all of a sudden. What's the secret?"

"No secret. I was just remembering how my mother had a wise saying for every occasion and how my dad always had an opposing adage. That way I had a choice."

"I knew you had to have inherited that argumentative nature from one of your parents."

She wrinkled her nose in protest. "Actually I didn't inherit that. Dad kept it all for himself. I'm sure there are times Mom wishes he could give it away, to me or anyone else."

"Not a marriage made in heaven, I take it."

"Oh, I wouldn't say that. They just have regular differences of opinion."

"Like us?" His tone was no longer light; it was a serious question. "We seem to have regular differences of opinion too."

Kylie kept her eyes straight ahead. "There's no comparison, Nick. My parents have been married for thirty years. Their disagreements are only superficial."

"And you think ours are not?"

Her breathing slowed with uncertainty. "I don't know, Nick. I think we're very different in some important ways."

"That isn't necessarily bad, you know." His voice was soft and reassuring, and she could feel the caress of his eyes. "As Spencer Tracy once said to Katharine Hepburn, *vive la différence!*"

Her smile was forced. She couldn't find amusement in something that was so important to her. She and Nick *were* different, and although that wasn't necessarily bad, it wasn't necessarily good either.

"You know," Nick said in a conversational tone, "I don't believe I've ever seen two people as different as Stephanie and Alex, yet they seem oddly suited to each other."

"Oddly?" Kylie asked, not really interested in a discussion of Stephanie and Alex, but not sure that she was up to a personal discussion of herself and Nick either.

"Well, they're very different in temperament and personality, but their individual differences could complement each other. Don't you think so?"

135

"It's a little early to tell. I think Alex needs someone to depend on him, someone who needs him. And for whatever reasons Stephanie needs Alex."

"Or at least she did before she became so assertive."

Kylie gave him an indignant look. "Being assertive doesn't negate a man or a woman's ability to relate to another person. Stephanie has just learned that Alex has to respect her as a person before he can ever feel anything for her as a woman."

"Do you really believe it's possible to separate gender from a relationship that is based on the unique differences between a man and a woman?"

"I believe mutual respect is the only basis for a fulfilling and lasting relationship."

Nick's mouth formed a curious upward slant. "Isn't that amazing? I find myself in complete agreement with you, Kylie. Do you think that's a good sign?"

"For what?"

"For future discussions about subjects that aren't superficial."

Her breath caught, and she wondered if they were about to embark on such a discussion. It seemed suddenly frightening and too soon. "I think that sounds like a trick question," she answered, impulsively opting for a lighter tone of voice and mood.

"No tricks. Would you like me to explain?"

Kylie hesitated, afraid he would ask her how she felt about commitment, afraid he wouldn't. "I—don't think so. Not now."

Nick respected her wish and didn't offer further comment. The silence wasn't as relaxed as during their earlier drive. It was heavy with emotion, with thoughts and feelings that Kylie didn't know how to express. The scenery she'd found so delightful before passed the car window in a meaningless blur of color. She was looking past the view

136

to a future with Nick, a future that beckoned her to take a chance. But did she dare risk her carefully mapped-out plans in the hope that Nick would accept her as an equal partner in their relationship? It was possible that he would want to make the decisions, take responsibility for her, as he had done for his mother. Would he expect her to meekly accept the role he chose for her?

Kylie smiled to herself. No, he knew she would never be meek, and she felt confident he wouldn't want her to be. Was her worrying pointless? Or was she really worried about her own uncertainties? Did she dare to acknowledge her own longing to depend on someone, her need for a man strong enough to support her in her quest to become all she could be?

She stole a glance at his attractive profile. How could she not take the chance? Nick was so much more than she'd ever hoped to find. She admired him, respected him. Loved him, her heart added, and Kylie didn't argue. It was certainly a foundation to build on. At least it would be, if he asked—

Nick heard Kylie's quiet sigh of indecision and wished he dared to ask her what she was thinking. He tightened his grip on the steering wheel. Hell! He wished he could ask her more than that.

He wanted to know how she felt about things like commitment, marriage—him. But it was too soon. She was uncertain. He knew that, but still he was tempted to force a decision about the future, their future. Even so, if Kylie needed more time, he wouldn't rush her.

As Nick guided the car into the drive of the company house, Kylie let her gaze touch him in an unguarded caress. *I love you, Nick.* The thought drifted into her mind like the beginning of a poem she had always known and yet had just now remembered, a gentle awakening to a time for decision.

She and Nick needed to talk about the future, about hopes and dreams and plans. But what if Nick didn't want to discuss it? With a decisive sigh Kylie leaned back and comforted herself with some of her father's timely advice: Nothing ventured, nothing gained.

CHAPTER EIGHT

As the car pulled to a stop beside a black Porsche parked slightly askew in the drive, Kylie straightened and glanced at Nick. "Isn't that Alex's car?"

Nick's smooth brow creased worriedly. "Yes, but I can't imagine why he would make a trip out here on a Saturday. On the weekends Alex usually avoids anything that has even a remote connection with the company."

"He could be here to see me, you know." Kylie tugged at the handle and pushed open the door, not waiting for Nick to open it for her. "You'll have to admit I'm more of an attraction than you are."

"I'll admit nothing of the sort," he said as he came around the front of the car to her side. "There are attractions and there are attractions, Miss Richards. Probably Alex wants to borrow my polka-dot tie or my chrome-plated tie clip or some such thing."

"He certainly won't want to borrow your taste if that's an example of your discrimination."

Nick captured her hand and led her toward the porch. "Oh, I don't know. He seems to like my discriminating taste in women. But don't worry, I almost never loan one out."

Kylie smiled serenely. "I wasn't worried at all. I can handle both Alex and his cousin."

"Pretty sure of yourself, aren't you? Would you like to put that statement, minus the part about handling Alex, of course, to the test? I know I would . . ." Nick's words trailed off as the solitary figure at the end of the porch came forward.

Stephanie turned apprehensive eyes first to Nick then to Kylie. "Hello," she said, her tone as overly bright as her eyes. "You're back."

"Hello, Stephanie." Kylie started up the stairs, wondering at the odd greeting. "Did we miss an appointment or something?"

"Have you been waiting for us?" Nick asked in a crisp but friendly voice. His gaze traveled past her to the closed door of the house. "Is Alex around here someplace?"

"No. I mean, yes. But Alex isn't—" The words gave way to a nervous smile, and Kylie noticed the agitated movement of Stephanie's hands. "Alex is—he's at the mill."

"What's happened?" Nick stepped onto the porch, concern etched in his features, his body tensed, alert. "Is something wrong?"

"No," Stephanie said quickly. "Nothing has happened —Alex just didn't want you to worry."

Nick took a deep breath before he turned to exchange a puzzled look with Kylie. "Let me get this straight, Stephanie," he said evenly. "Nothing has happened. Alex is at the mill—on a Saturday—and he sent you here—in his Porsche—to tell me that nothing has happened just so I wouldn't worry. Right?"

Stephanie's pallor made her eyes seem unnaturally blue as she faced Nick squarely. "No, Mr. Braden—Nick, that

isn't right. That's what Alex wanted me to tell you, but—"
She paused, loyalty to Southwest weighing in the balance
against her desire to please Alex. "I think maybe it would
be better if you joined him there."

"At the mill?" Nick asked. "Is anyone hurt?"

Kylie had to admire his restraint and patience with
Stephanie's vague responses.

"Oh, no, nothing like that has happened." Stephanie
shook her head to emphasize the denial. "It's just—well,
Alex will tell you."

With a nod Nick met Kylie's eyes briefly. Then he was
striding, in a running walk, away from the house toward
the driveway.

With a lingering gaze Kylie watched him before turning
to smile at Stephanie. "How about something to drink?"

"Oh, please." Stephanie seemed intent on watching
Nick's departure too. "I hope I—" The blue eyes came to
rest on Kylie with sad appeal. "Could we talk?"

"Of course. Let's go inside." Kylie reined in her rampant curiosity to give the other woman a chance to regain
some much-needed composure. But once inside, as they
sat in the living area beside tall glasses of iced tea, the
silence was frustratingly long. Finally, just when she
thought she couldn't take another minute, Kylie heard a
soft heartfelt sigh.

"He'll never forgive me for sending Nick." Stephanie
leaned her head against the back of the sofa in a gesture
of defeat. "But I had to do it. You understand, don't you,
Kylie?"

"I'm sure I will if you'll start at the beginning and tell
me what happened."

"Okay, but I'm not sure of the details myself. Alex
called a few hours ago and told me to meet him at the
office. I told him I didn't work on the weekend and that
whatever he had for me to do could wait until Monday.

141

But then he said, 'I need you here. Please come, Stephanie.' " Again she emitted that deep sigh. "It was the first time he'd ever called me by my name, and well, I had to do as he asked."

"I can understand that." Kylie offered the only comfort she thought might be acceptable at the moment. "But what happened at the mill?"

"A fire. Alex wouldn't let me go inside the building, but he said it was minor and there wasn't much damage. There was a fire truck and several of our own security people, and no one seemed greatly alarmed. Alex was positive, though, that somehow Nick would hear about it over the radio or something, and he sent me to break the news."

Stephanie rubbed her temples wearily. "I didn't do a very good job of that, did I? No telling what Nick thought, but—Alex told me he didn't want his cousin anywhere near the plant, that I should make sure Nick stayed right here and waited for his call."

Kylie frowned in confusion. "Why would Alex ask you to do something like that? A minor fire is not a major catastrophe, but Nick would need to know. And he would want to see for himself, just for his own reassurance. I mean, accidents happen sometimes—"

"It wasn't an accident, Kylie," Stephanie interrupted. "Alex said it looked like arson, and he—he didn't want Nick to know that. That's why he sent me. He thought he could disguise the evidence somehow. I tried to tell him it wasn't possible. I mean, there were people all around. But Alex seemed to think he could keep Nick from finding out and laying the blame on him."

"Nick wouldn't do that. Alex can't be held responsible for everything that goes wrong at Southwest."

"But Alex does feel responsible for everything that goes wrong. He could be a really fine executive, you know, if

142

his family would leave him alone. But they seem to delight in criticizing his every decision, every idea."

"Stephanie, if concealing evidence in a fire is an example of his ideas and ability to make mature decisions, he needs more than criticism."

"That's easy for you to say, Kylie." Stephanie sat up, defensiveness written in every angle of her body. "No one is going to hold you accountable for today's fire. And no one will expect you to explain how and why such a thing happened."

"He is the president of the company," Kylie said, trying to insert some reason into the building ferocity of Stephanie's argument. "And the president of any company is expected to investigate and explain—"

"Alex could do that," Stephanie interrupted vigorously. "If Nick wasn't here breathing down his neck, Alex would conduct an investigation, and he'd get to the bottom of this in no time." She paused, and her eyes shone with conviction. "He just needs the chance to prove he's capable of handling the responsibility of his position, to feel proud of his accomplishments and to learn from his own mistakes. Surely everyone is entitled to that. You said so in the first training session, didn't you, Kylie?"

Blinking at the barrage of wisdom—her own wisdom, evidently—Kylie was at a loss for words. She could only wonder at the idiosyncrasies of human nature. The traits others interpreted as weakness in Alex Jamison, Stephanie, seeing with love's vision, understood as potential strengths.

Nick was right, Kylie thought. The differences between two people weren't necessarily bad. And in this case they seemed good and very right. Alex needed someone to believe in him, and Stephanie needed someone to believe in. Suddenly Kylie felt that the future was a kaleidoscope of promise.

"You don't think Alex can handle the job either," Stephanie said, obviously interpreting the silence as a negative response. "But you're wrong, Kylie. If Nick will just leave him alone—"

"Don't blame Nick." Kylie knew her voice was sharp, but she couldn't hold back the defensive retort. "If Alex can handle the job, Stephanie, he can do so with or without someone breathing down his neck, as you put it. Nick is simply doing his job."

"I should have known you'd take that attitude. No one is ever on Alex's side."

Kylie took a deep breath and refrained from mentioning that there was probably a good reason for that. Instead she reminded herself that Stephanie was upset by the afternoon's events and forced a smile. "With you on his side he doesn't appear to need anyone else."

Stephanie managed an equally forced smile and lapsed into an uneasy silence. Kylie ignored her iced drink to stare out the patio doors as a restlessness settled around her. Finally, deciding that Stephanie was no more in the mood for conversation than she was, Kylie excused herself and went to her bedroom to change clothes.

She was tempted to take a soothing soak in the tub, but she contented herself with a brief hot shower and a brisk rubdown. As she slipped into the brightly colored folds of a caftan, she thought of Nick and wondered what he was doing. Taking charge, more than likely, she thought confidently. Bringing some semblance of order to a disorderly situation.

Nick. She savored the thought of him and cradled within her heart the knowledge of her love for him. Everything was going to work out beautifully. As soon as she finished the seminar—The seminar! Apprehension prickled along her spine. Trouble at the mill could mean trouble for her seminar too. But, no, it was silly even to consider the idea.

One thing was not indicative of the other, and Nick wouldn't—

Of course he wouldn't. Resolutely Kylie pushed the negative thoughts from her mind, brushed her chestnut curls, and joined a still-pensive Stephanie in the living area.

But the doubts remained at the edge of her consciousness until the moment Nick walked into the room. He looked tired, drained, but her fears receded at the reassuring slant of his lips.

Alex's perpetual good humor was not in evidence, Kylie noted. As he followed Nick into the room Alex smiled, but it was a weak attempt at best and only emphasized the lines of strain in his face. Without waiting for a greeting Stephanie moved to his side and slipped her hand into his. Alex looked down at his secretary with an oddly surprised expression.

"Everything is all right, isn't it?" Stephanie said softly, making it a combination of question and statement.

Alex nodded, his whole attention focused on the woman who was staring up at him with such quiet confidence. Kylie felt suddenly awkward watching them, and her eyes sought Nick's to see if he, too, felt like an intruder on a private moment.

But if Nick had any such feelings, he was hiding them admirably. In fact, he seemed far more interested in Kylie's untouched glass of tea on the coffee table. With a wry shake of her head Kylie walked to the table, lifted the glass, and motioned for Nick to follow her into the kitchen.

"Is everything all right?" she asked when they were safely out of earshot.

Nick leaned against the counter, his gaze on her as she filled a clean glass with ice cubes. "Well, that all depends on your point of view. Everything at the plant is under

145

control. The fire safety equipment we installed worked perfectly, so the damage is minor. A few hours of clean up and a couple of repairs should get things back in order. I just wish the other problems could be cleaned up as easily."

Kylie poured tea into the glass and offered it to him. "I'm almost afraid to ask what the other problems are."

Staring down at the iced drink in his hands, Nick emitted a weary sigh. "Alex has made a big mistake this time, Kylie. Grandfather is going to hit the roof, and I don't think even Aunt Rosemary will be able to charm him down."

"Stephanie told me she tried to talk Alex out of concealing the evidence, but he was adamant. I can't imagine how he thought he could hide something like arson from you or anyone else."

"Arson?" Nick asked sharply. "God, is that what he told her? It wasn't arson, Kylie. It was negligence. Alex's own negligence. He's responsible for the storage and disposal of the chemicals used at Southwest, probably the most important safety precaution in the entire plant. The chemicals were in the wrong place. *The wrong place,* Kylie. Do you realize what could have happened if the fire had started during the workweek, when that building housed a full shift of employees and not just a few maintenance people?"

"Disaster." Her whispered word hung heavily in the air, and she wished for Stephanie's sake that there might be a mistake. "You're sure it was his fault?"

Nick's gray eyes spoke volumes in a brief glance. "I'm sure. If Alex had conducted even one of the checks he's supposed to make during the week, he would have discovered the error."

"I guess nothing like this has ever happened before?"

"Not to my knowledge," Nick said, placing his glass on

the counter. "But then, Stephanie never left Alex completely on his own before—"

"Before my seminar," Kylie finished the sentence with a frown. "Poor Stephanie. Just when things were beginning to look promising."

"If you're going to start dispensing sympathy, save some for me. I'm the one who's caught in between family ties and business ethics." Nick reached for her hand and pulled her into his arms with a smooth tug.

"Nick, we have company." Kylie made a weak protest even as her arms wound around his neck.

"That sounds very domestic, Kylie, but I'm just not in the mood for entertaining."

As if on cue there came the sound of a car door closing and then the muffled hum of Alex's Porsche. Nick smiled. "I guess our company wasn't in the mood to be entertained either."

"How convenient," Kylie murmured, lifting her lips to invite his kiss.

He accepted her offer with a touch that was almost rough in its intensity. The coolness of the iced tea lingered on his lips, and she pressed closer to warm him. His tongue invaded her mouth as he molded her resilient body to his own. Desire whispered through her with aching urgency, and she shivered with longing.

Wanting him had become such a part of her that he could summon it from her at will. Just a touch, a word, a look, and her love for him responded. But this time Kylie felt he needed something more from her. Intuitively she knew he was seeking comfort in her arms, a quiet place to retreat from the responsibilities that weighed so heavily on him. At the thought a sweet sense of contentment settled within her, and she gave herself up to the fulfillment of his kiss.

Nick cradled her against him and buried his face in the

softness of her hair. "You smell wonderful. I'm going to miss that musky perfume you wear."

"Miss?" she asked absently. "Are you going somewhere?"

"San Francisco, first thing in the morning. I have to drive into Albuquerque to catch a direct flight, so I'll have to leave early. If you'll get packed tonight and go with me, you can probably get a direct flight to San Diego, and we'll have a few extra hours together."

"I don't need a flight to San Diego, direct or otherwise." Kylie tilted her face back to look into his eyes. "But I might be persuaded to get up early enough to have breakfast with you."

His hands found her shoulders and tightened their hold. "You're returning home tomorrow, Kylie. With no arguments."

"Why?" She stepped back, separating herself from him by a small but important distance.

"You're going home because I said so—because that's what I want."

Displeasure stiffened her posture. "And what if it isn't what I want, Nick?"

"Don't be difficult about this, Kylie."

"Just how do you want me to be? Meek and obedient? I'm not, you know."

"I know." He released her from his grasp. "You're assertive and independent. You're also argumentative and unreasonable at times."

"Unreasonable? Simply because I won't obey your order? I have a training seminar to complete, Nick, and I see no reason to stop it now."

His mouth formed a derisive line. "I don't suppose a simple request from me would be sufficient cause?"

"No." She stepped back, increasing the space between them as if she were drawing boundary lines. "And please don't put me in a position where I'm torn between personal wishes and professional commitments."

"I'm afraid that can't be helped, Kylie. You can choose to leave Santa Fe because I asked you as a personal favor, or you can leave because I relieved you of your professional duties. But either way you're leaving."

She made a futile attempt to control her temper. "I believe we've had this discussion before, Nick. I have a contract, and I intend to hold you to it."

"Kylie," he said with an entreating look, "please try to understand. I should never have allowed you to begin the seminar in the first place, but now . . ."

His voice drifted into an uneasy pause, and her anger focused with chilling purpose. "But now? Now what, Nick? You can't believe the assertiveness training had anything to do with the fire today." She stopped, tensely waiting for him to deny it. The silence was suffocating. "That's what you think, isn't it? You honestly think I'm respon—" Her throat closed around the word as she met his eyes.

"No! Stop it, Kylie. You know that isn't true. But the seminar certainly might have influenced—"

"You *do* blame the seminar!" She turned away in disgust, but he caught her arm and jerked her around to face him.

"That isn't what I said, damn it! Listen to me. Your blasted training sessions are responsible for a lot of changes taking place at Southwest."

"Good changes, Nick," she interrupted.

"That remains to be seen. At any rate, if Stephanie hadn't been attending your seminars and had monitored Alex's safety checks as she usually did, then maybe—and I mean *maybe*—the fire might not have happened." He released his grip on her and raked his fingers through his hair. "God, now I'm making excuses for Alex. I don't want to argue with you, Kylie, but I can't let you stay."

"I'm staying."

A muscle in his jaw clenched with the effort to remain calm. "The repercussions of this incident are just beginning. There's no way to tell what might happen at this point."

"That sounds fatalistically ominous, Nick. What could happen?"

"Word of the fire and its cause will be all over the plant by Monday morning. Demands for a change in management will be rampant. An incident of negligence that endangers the well-being of employees can be explosive. The employees have a right to an explanation, and with all the crazy assertiveness principles you've been feeding them, there could be no end to the trouble—"

"*Crazy* assertiveness principles?" Kylie didn't know how she kept her voice from shaking with anger.

His lean fingers massaged his temple for a moment. "Look, I didn't mean—well, maybe I did. Sometimes I think you're crazy to believe in those ridiculous principles, and sometimes I think I'm crazy not to. But right now I just don't have time to meditate on your theories. The way it stands, I'm going to have a hell of a time explaining to my grandfather why I didn't fire you in the beginning. And it's going to be even worse convincing Aunt Rosemary that your seminar isn't directly responsible for Alex's disastrous mistake."

"If you're my only advocate, I'm afraid it's a lost cause already," she drawled sarcastically. "The best argument for my seminar will be the production report at the end of the quarter. And did it ever occur to you that if I continue the training course, it could defuse the explosive situation you're anticipating? Let me finish the seminar, Nick, and prove its value—even to your satisfaction."

150

"I can't do that. Not after what happened today. Now at best your seminar will become a platform for discontented, loud employees who want a place to be heard. And at worst it could provoke a full-fledged mutiny. I've seen that kind of thing happen, Kylie. After much less significant incidents."

"Didn't you listen to what I just said, Nick? That's the very reason I should continue the training course. I'm teaching a way of thinking that can change a negative situation into a positive one. Your employees need to know that their opinions count, and my training will show them positive ways to express those opinions. The best thing you can do now is to allow the seminar to go on as usual. No break in routine. It will work for you, Nick. I know it will. Just let me—"

"Contrary to what you may think, Kylie, I do have some experience with assertiveness training. It can get out of control. And under these circumstances, well, I just can't take the chance on that happening here—with you."

"It won't happen, Nick. You'll see—"

"I won't see, because there will be no more seminar. It's just too chancy. I can't be here to monitor the sessions, and I don't have time to worry about what might be happening in my absence. You're going home."

Monitoring? Kylie could hardly believe it. All the time she'd thought his presence at the seminar indicated his interest in what she had to say. But instead he'd been monitoring employee reaction, ready to rescue her should anything get out of hand.

"I don't need your protection, Nick," she said coolly. "And I don't need you to order me home like a rebellious child. I am not in any way responsible for the problems you have at Southwest, and you won't treat me as if I am. You may have the authority to cancel the sessions, Nick, and you can certainly order me to leave your house, but you can't force me to leave Santa Fe. I'm staying whether you like it or not."

"You'll do as you're told," he said tightly and knew immediately it was the worst possible thing he could have said to her. But damn, what did she expect? He'd spent a terrible afternoon trying to straighten out the mess Alex had made. And in a few hours he had to face a family row that would rage for days. The last thing he needed right now was Kylie's complete disregard for his judgment.

God, would she never stop fighting him? He watched her eyes darken, watched the stubborn tilt of her chin, and made himself repeat the hollow command. "You'll do as you're told." Resolutely he resisted the impulse to add "please."

Kylie straightened her shoulders and faced him, anger seeming to add to her stature. "I haven't done what I've been told to do for a very long time, Nick. I don't take orders, and I certainly don't need anyone to make decisions for me, least of all you."

She might have imagined the bleak look that appeared in his eyes, but she couldn't miss the chilling appraisal that followed it.

"Apparently you don't need me for any reason, Kylie. So if you'll excuse me, I have more important things to do." He walked past her, taking obvious care not to touch her in even the most casual way.

She waited, hoping vaguely for the sound of a slamming door. Something, anything that would show some emotion, take the sting from his last indifferent remark. But there was no sound from the inner sanctum of the house, and somehow that seemed frighteningly final.

It was all his fault, she thought as she absently rinsed his glass and put it in the dishwasher. Blaming her for Alex's mistake was unforgivable. And Nick's whole attitude about the seminar was prejudiced and autocratic. If he would just once listen to her with an open mind—

Kylie frowned at her attempts to rationalize her position. In all honesty she hadn't done much listening to his point of view either. Of course, in this case she was in the right, but still she could have considered his feelings. Nick was torn by the unfair expectations of his family. He was trying to make the best of a bad situation, and she had done everything she could to make it worse. Somehow knowing she was in the right didn't make her feel better.

The fact remained that Nick was leaving. He was probably packing at this very minute. And God only knew when she would see him again. The very thought shriveled inside her. How many empty days before he would return to her? Or would he return at all? She certainly hadn't given him any reason to suppose he'd be welcome. What if—?

She couldn't face the question, much less the answer, and decisively she turned to the door. *You don't need me.* His words rang in her ears, mocking all arguments against going to him. She couldn't let him leave believing such a lie. She needed him desperately, in so many ways. There had to be some way to show him that, despite their differences of opinion, she loved him, needed him.

"Nick?" Kylie prefaced her entrance into his bedroom with the question. "Nick?" she called again as she stepped inside and found the room empty. A suitcase lay open on the bed, and Kylie averted her gaze, feeling the loneliness that already seemed to be settling over the house and her.

"Need something?" Nick's drawl was dry and not at all encouraging.

Her gaze swung toward the bathroom doorway, where he stood, minus shoes, socks, and shirt. His hair was mussed in the most appealing way, and the muscled expanse of his chest beckoned to her senses. Kylie clasped

153

her hands behind her to keep from following them into his arms—a place where she wouldn't be welcome at the moment.

"I—uh—thought we might . . . talk," she suggested hesitantly.

The quick lift of his brows expressed his opinion even before he discouraged any further suggestions by closing the bathroom door. Kylie stared at the door, took a step forward, stopped, took another step, and finally touched the knob before her courage failed entirely.

Think positive. Be assertive. The thoughts came easily, but opening the door that separated her from Nick proved to be more difficult. And when at last she managed to push it open, it took all her effort not to close it again.

From mirrored tiles to sunken tub to the see-through shower panels, the room was an exact match for the bath that adjoined her bedroom. A match, that is, except for the man who stood, completely nude, with one foot inside the shower. Kylie couldn't control her unabashed stare, which traveled lingeringly from that one foot up and over his lean symmetry. A blush tinted her cheeks as she helplessly admired all that made him so devastatingly male.

Totally oblivious of her scrutiny, Nick glanced over his shoulder and shook his head. "If you want to take a shower, Kylie, you'll have to wait your turn."

"I . . . I'm not very good at waiting." She tried for the most nonchalant tone in her repertoire and knew she fell far short of the goal. "And I don't want a shower. I want . . ."—pausing, she swallowed hard—"you."

His eyes darkened perceptibly. "And I want . . ."—the words trailed into a husky whisper, and Kylie waited breathlessly—"a shower."

It took a full minute before her mind registered that what she'd heard was not what she'd expected to hear. The sound of water noisily slapping the glass walls aroused her temper. She could almost feel the spray prickling her skin with pinpoints of irritation. He had a hell of a nerve . . .

When she jerked open the shower door and felt the moistness on her face, Kylie considered the wisdom of following her impulse into action. But one look at the cool gray eyes regarding her with solemn expectation told her it was too late for a graceful retreat. Determination pushed a weak smile across her lips. "I . . . told you I wasn't very good at waiting," she offered faintly.

"Then by all means join me," he said with a sweeping gesture.

"Oh, no, I didn't . . . " she began even as his fingers closed around her wrist. With a firm tug he pulled her into the cubicle. "Nick, I'm dressed and . . . " The sentence drowned as he pushed her beneath the full force of the water. In a matter of seconds the caftan was plastered uselessly against her every curve.

Well, perhaps not so uselessly, she decided as she caught the subtle change in Nick's expression. Pushing the dripping hair from her eyes, she tried to turn her reproachful glare into a provocative look. "I only wanted to talk, Nick."

"I'm your captive audience." He reached past her for the soap, his forearm brushing against her breasts in the process. Her gasp was soft, but she knew by his sly smile that he had heard and correctly interpreted her reaction. His hands cupped the roundness of her shoulders and manuevered her away from the direct spray and himself beneath it. "Here," he said, placing the bar of soap in her hand. "While you talk make yourself useful. Wash my back." Then he turned so she could obey the command.

Kylie wanted to protest. In fact, she fully intended to protest, but at the sight of the unlimited opportunity before her, she forgot what she had intended to say. She rubbed the soap until her palms were frothy with lather. Then she reached past him to replace the soap, letting her arms imitate his action and brush seductively over his taut stomach before sliding around to his back and upward to his neck.

Her thumbs found the corded muscles at his nape and began a rhythmic massage. The ripple of pleasure he felt and resisted communicated itself to her through the sudden tension beneath her fingertips. Her lips curved with satisfaction and the temptation to test the limits of his resistance.

Slowly her hands massaged the lather onto his shoulders and down his back. The stinging spray washed the soap from him almost as quickly as she rubbed it on, leaving his skin satiny slick to the touch. With tiny, circling strokes she washed him until her fingers discovered the curve of his waist and moved lower to his hips. Unable to resist, Kylie stepped forward and pressed a moist kiss on the center of his back.

But when she tried to reinstate the distance between them, the saturated material of her caftan clung to Nick, rubbing sensuously against her breasts and refusing to release its damp bond on either side. Deciding that it was too much trouble to disentangle herself, she cupped her body to his and let her arms slide around his waist.

This time Kylie couldn't be sure whether the shiver of pleasure emanated from Nick or from within her. Her cheek tingled where it touched his skin, and the clean, wet taste of him was warm in her mouth.

The cascading water enveloped them in a steamy embrace, and the rapid beating of her heart duplicated the uneven pattern of his breathing. For several long seconds he stood passive, his hands covering hers, and then he turned in her arms and cradled her close.

Her lips investigated the wiry tendrils of hair on his

chest and discovered first one male nipple and then the other. She heard his quickly drawn breath and felt it echo in her throat as his fingers moved against the wet fabric covering her breast and began a stimulating massage.

Kylie sent her hands on a lingering exploration from his hips to the backs of his legs and around to the sensitive skin of his inner thighs. Tilting her head so she could look into his eyes, she allowed her fingers to touch him intimately, caressingly.

A groan rumbled in his throat. "I thought you wanted to talk," he said thickly.

"And I thought I was communicating rather well." Kylie smiled, reveling in the knowledge that he wanted her. "Nick, has anyone ever made love to you in the shower?" She paused. "On second thought, don't answer that."

He twisted a finger in the dripping curls at her temple. "I've never before been seduced by a water sprite in a sopping wet gown. I thought they wore only drip-dry."

"Actually," Kylie said, sliding her hands up the deep vee of dark chest hair to his shoulders, "water sprites wear nothing at all."

"Ahhh." He arched his brows knowingly. "Then let's dispense with your disguise."

Obediently her hands found the fastener of the caftan, but the material clung stubbornly to her skin. With a slow smile Nick slipped his fingers under the fabric and eased it down and over her shoulders. Kylie freed her arms while he took his time in the sensuously slow process of lifting the covering from her breasts. The stroking caress of his knuckles sent delicate tremors of longing through her.

Unable to remain still beneath his appreciative touch, she ran her fingertips the length of his arms and let them drop to the slight indentation above his hips. The caftan slithered downward and tangled around her legs. She twisted in an effort to be rid of the nuisance, but Nick stayed her struggle and bent to strip the material from her legs.

Heat spiraled through her as his hand encircled her ankle, lifting her foot and pulling the garment aside before repeating the action with the other foot. Then Nick began the lingering ascent, exploring every naked inch of her as he straightened. Cupping her breast in his palm, he breathed a caress at the corner of her mouth.

"You weren't wearing anything under that," he said huskily. "That shows definite premeditation, Kylie. No one would ever believe you came in here to talk."

The need to feel his lips on hers ached in her throat, and she lifted her hands to his face. "Don't you ever shut up, Nick?"

He answered with a forceful kiss that demanded her complete cooperation. And Kylie gave it. She wrapped her arms around his neck and parted her lips, letting her tongue initiate a more intimate union. Her damp skin bonded naturally to his, allying thigh to thigh and feminine curves to masculine angles.

Passion altered the atmosphere around her until Kylie thought that the steamy heat must be radiating from within her. When Nick moved, she moved with him, and it wasn't until the cool air struck her bare toes that she realized he had turned off the water and was carrying her from the shower.

Moisture began to evaporate from her skin, and she snuggled into his hold for warmth. She pressed a kiss in the hollow of his shoulder, liking the taste of the water droplets that rewarded her effort. Discovering the pleasure in this activity, her mouth returned for another sip, seeking out the tantalizing curves of his neck and the sensitive spot below his ear.

Kylie became entranced with the cadence of his pulse

beneath her lips. The rhythm throbbed into the depths of her emotions and returned to him in shimmering vibrations of desire. It felt good, so good that she wondered how she had survived before Nick's touch had awakened her and she had discovered how perfectly she fit into his embrace. Before her heart had found its missing piece.

Her arms tightened around his neck as he arrived at the bed and lowered her onto the mattress, but he pulled free of her touch and reached over her to shove the suitcase out of the way. Silky lashes drifted down to shield her from the reminder of imminent separation. She wouldn't think of empty days and nights. She couldn't bear to think of empty arms.

Not now. Not when she could feel the warmth of him so close. Not when his scent was so deliciously near. Not when she could open her eyes and drink in the sight of him. Her hands lifted to him in silent supplication.

And then he was beside her, his body a shelter for her uncertainties, his lips a soothing draught of forgetfulness. Her senses swelled with wanting him, and her fingertips traced damp patterns across his shoulders.

When his mouth closed over the rosy invitation of her breast, Kylie shivered beneath the caress. As she moved her head back and forth against the satin coverlet, her hair splayed across the bed in silky wet strands. In some vague mist of awareness she realized that she and Nick hadn't bothered with even the thought of drying the moisture that clung to them.

"Nick," she whispered huskily, "the spread is getting all wet."

With a total lack of concern for the state of the spread, Nick etched tiny spirals with his tongue over the slope of her breasts to the softly shadowed cleft between. His lips sent tender yearnings flooding through her mind as he worked his way up to the hollow of her throat and then hovered only a breath away from her mouth. "Just pretend you're in the middle of a mountain stream . . . with me."

He sealed the image with a kiss, but Kylie knew there was no need for pretense. The reality was too beautiful, too wonderfully right for imaginings.

His breath mingled with hers as he claimed possession of her, and she gave herself completely to the wild winds of heaven that whirled through her. Her body was his to command, just as her heart was his to keep. For all her hard-won independence she needed Nick, would always need him.

With a final, willing sigh of surrender she released her love for him and felt it soar, free of doubt, into a realm of promise.

CHAPTER NINE

Morning came in varied segments of dreamy sensation. Kylie savored the slow awakening in Nick's arms, absorbing the warm, sleepy scent of him and the delicious roughness of his body curled drowsily around hers. The travel clock beside the bed ticked mercilessly, counting off the seconds.

A sigh built in her throat, but Kylie held it in check. She didn't want to disturb Nick's rest by even the slightest alteration of her breathing. In an hour he would be on his way to San Francisco, and she wanted this time just for herself.

Wrapped in the intimacy of the silent house, she felt a secret delight in watching him. Sleep-tumbled dark hair lay across his forehead, and his chiseled features were relaxed and gentled. Her fingertip tingled with the desire to touch the laugh lines at the outer corners of his eyes. But she denied herself the tactile satisfaction, letting her gaze trace the lines instead and imprint them for all time on her memory.

She wanted to be able to remember how it felt to be so

161

near to him, to summon at will the sweet seduction of her senses that even now suffused her with longing. How could she bear to remain in this empty house without him, separated by miles and the unresolved situation between them?

It would be wonderful if he asked her to accompany him, asked her to come home with him and meet his family. Kylie smiled softly at the old-fashioned thought. But even if he asked, she knew she couldn't go. She had to complete the seminar.

The silence was shattered by a high-pitched alarm, and Kylie watched with tender amusement as Nick struggled awake. He groped for the clock and in a matter of seconds restored quiet. "Damn," he muttered thickly. "It's morning."

"A very beautiful morning." She leaned toward him and greeted his lips with a butterfly touch.

His hand curved at her nape and insisted on a more thorough kiss. "I see what you mean," he said as he drew back from her mouth.

Kylie smiled into his gray eyes cloudy with dreams. "Good morning."

"Hmmm. Good morning." He punctuated the words with another kiss, a deeper, more demanding kiss, which invaded her senses.

She pressed into him with the faint hope of postponing the impending separation. A slow shudder ran the length of the arm that embraced her, and then Nick reluctantly, regretfully released her. "I'm already dreading tomorrow, when you won't be there to wake me."

"There's a simple solution," Kylie said. "I'll just phone you first thing in the morning . . . at your expense of course."

His deep sigh reflected her own lack of enthusiasm for the idea. "Somehow I don't think it would be a very

162

satisfying substitute, but I suppose it's my only choice." He turned to look at the time and groaned. "Did I set that blasted alarm or did you?"

Kylie nestled in the curve of his arm, hungry for just a few more minutes of his undivided attention. "Yes," she said simply.

"Yes, what?" he asked, his breath stirring her disheveled curls.

"Yes, you set it, and yes, I reset it. I thought you needed an extra hour's rest more than you needed breakfast."

"That was a damned impertinent thing to do, Kylie. Especially since I needed an extra hour with you more than I needed either rest or breakfast."

"Considering your rather unpleasant disposition this morning, perhaps you need a cold shower."

"Only if you'll heat the water for me as you did last night." He placed a provocative kiss at the arch of her brow and then made a smooth foray down the bridge of her nose until he could capture her lips.

Suddenly Nick's manner was no longer teasing, and Kylie shifted to curve her arms around him and return his caress with an urgency born of loving. Never had she thought she would ache with the mere idea of being apart from someone.

His hands moved over her in long, searching strokes, as if trying to soften the almost desperate intensity of their embrace. She felt him struggle to regain control and tried to master her own runaway desire.

"Kylie," he whispered at last, his voice husky with emotion. "God, I don't want to leave you. I wish—" He rolled to the edge of the bed and swung his feet to the floor. He stood, the muscles of his back displaying his tension. "I can't miss that plane, Kylie."

He made a slow turn, and she felt the heat of his gaze on her, felt the strength of his desire and the tremendous effort of will he exercised in not physically touching her. "Maybe I'll try that cold shower after all."

She watched him walk from the room, heard the bathroom door close, and lay back against the tousled sheets. A cold shower wouldn't be a bad idea for her either, she thought with a sigh. Why on earth had she reset the alarm? Had she really been so satiated with loving that she hadn't realized desire would be born anew with the dawn?

Maybe subconsciously she had wanted this first goodbye to be brief and dissatisfying in the hopes it would speed his return. But it was too late for regrets. There just wasn't time. And now she had no choice but to be glad for these few minutes alone to compose herself. At least Nick wouldn't carry the image of a love-sick, sad-eyed woman with him to San Francisco. She would make sure of that.

In the bathroom Nick eyed his reflection in disgust. He was acting like some love-sick kid going off to college and leaving his high school sweetheart behind. And he hadn't experienced such a failure of self-restraint in years. Of course he'd never before experienced anything close to the feelings Kylie aroused in him.

Kylie. The thought of her was a quiet ache inside him.

Nick gave the faucet a frustrated twist and bent to splash the cool water on his face. Rubbing the moisture away, he frowned into the mirror. "You can't take her with you, Braden," he said aloud. "You know you can't take her with you."

He knew it was true. The next few days would leave little time to spend with her in any case. He would be thoroughly immersed in the battle that was probably raging at this very moment. Not exactly a great time to introduce Kylie to the family. What would she think of his grandfather's authoritarian approach to any argument? he wondered. And would she be as overwhelmed by his aunt as most people were?

Nick allowed himself the luxury of imagining Kylie's reaction. With her assertiveness principles and progressive theories she would probably stir up more controversy than he could handle. He felt relatively certain that neither his grandfather nor his aunt would be open-minded and understanding about Kylie's spirit at this particular time.

He could depend on his mother to welcome her, of course, but what Kylie's reaction to such a gentle, unassertive woman would be Nick couldn't predict. No. He stopped the speculation cold. This was simply the wrong time to take Kylie home. Besides, he knew she wasn't leaving Santa Fe, and they still hadn't settled the issue of that damn seminar. It was better for all concerned to wait until the situation was resolved.

By the time he'd dressed and finished packing, Nick had reluctantly convinced himself of the wisdom of his decision. At least he was convinced right up to the minute he put his luggage into the car and turned to say good-bye.

Kylie slipped into his arms with a determined smile. "Don't forget to write," she quipped.

"I hope to be back before the pony express could deliver a letter." His voice was as resolutely cheerful as her own. "Don't cause any trouble while I'm gone, okay?"

"Is that an order or a request?"

"Just a heartfelt wish." Nick tightened his hold on her. "Kylie," he began almost hesitantly, "put the seminar on hold for now . . . please. I know you're going to stay here. But do some sight-seeing. Relax and enjoy a vacation . . . at my expense. As soon as this mess with Alex is straightened out, we'll talk."

"Nick, I know you're worried about the situation here, but you don't have to be. I can help, really I can. By continuing the training course I can help to keep the employees communicating with management. You don't have to fight on two fronts. You handle the home office

165

and let me handle things here. Don't ask me to stop the seminar now." Kylie had used all her powers of persuasion, and now she willed him to agree, but she knew by the look in his eyes that he still didn't believe her.

His thumb stroked her cheek, and his mouth formed a wistful line. "I am asking, Kylie. Please don't refuse."

She couldn't in good conscience agree, but she simply couldn't find the words to refuse either. Finally her desire for a harmonious parting won out, and with a sigh she nodded. "All right, Nick. But only for a while."

He accepted the compromise by brushing a finger across her lips. His farewell kiss was tender. His good-bye was a throaty whisper that Kylie knew would echo hauntingly in her every dream. She watched until the car was out of sight before returning to the house and the prospect of a totally unappealing vacation.

During the next few days Kylie saw more of Santa Fe and the surrounding area than she really wanted to see. She had lunch with Stephanie and heard more than she wanted to hear about Alex. She had dinner with a very subdued Alex and discovered more than she wanted to know about his sudden, inexplicable attraction to brunettes.

The hours were busy with activities, yet Kylie felt as if she were constantly waiting. Waiting for night to ease her empty arms with sleep, waiting for sunrise to ease her empty dreams with wakefulness. Waiting for Nick's calls, which both appeased her longing and increased her dissatisfaction.

Loneliness is a state of mind, she told herself again and again, but she finally admitted that loneliness was a state of heart and therefore completely immune to logic.

By the end of the week Kylie had had her fill of leisurely activity. She found herself in her office at Southwest, thumbing through notes and chafing at the inopportune interruption of the seminar. Nick had made a mistake in canceling the sessions. The tension among the employees was almost palpable, and several times, as she walked through the building, she'd been asked when the training course would continue.

Whether he realized it or not, Nick had only heightened speculation among the employees, and Kylie was utterly frustrated by the knowledge that she could have helped to ease the strained situation.

Alex reinforced her frustration at every turn. He seemed quietly resigned since the fire, as if he were waiting for the verdict. Kylie discovered that, stripped of his arrogant self-confidence, Alex exhibited some of the likable character traits that Stephanie had known about all along. More than anything else Kylie regretted that now, when Alex was receptive and needed assertiveness training, the seminar was on hold.

Alex wasn't happy about the delay and told her more than once that she should consider resuming the sessions. She resisted the temptation, though, reminding herself of Nick's request. But as the days wore on and she sensed the growing restlessness at the mill, Kylie began to consider Alex's suggestion.

Nick would disapprove. She had little doubt of that. But Nick was in California. A long way from the situation, and after all, she had told him before he left that the delay was temporary. He knew she had every intention of finishing the seminar when he returned. And each day that she allowed the delay to continue, she lost some of the trainees' initial enthusiasm for the course.

When Alex told her in a tremulous but nonetheless authoritative voice that he wanted her to begin the sessions again the following week, Kylie was eager to agree. Despite his assurances that he would take the responsibility of apprising Nick and the home office, she decided to mention it to Nick herself.

Nick might not be thrilled with the information, but Kylie hoped he would go along with her. Besides, by now he had surely had time to consider the matter from her perspective and could agree that continuing the seminar would be best for all concerned. And even if he didn't agree with her, it might be the catalyst that brought him back to her.

He had given no indication of when he might return. At first he had telephoned every evening, but the phone had been sullenly silent for the past two days. Well, Kylie decided, there was no reason she couldn't phone him. And she would.

Procrastination became the byword during the weekend, though, as she allowed one thing after another to postpone that call. But when the·sun set on a lazy Sunday, Kylie gathered her courage in one hand and lifted the telephone receiver in the other.

Nick closed the door and tossed his keys onto the table in the entryway of his apartment. The telephone shrilled a summons that he was sorely tempted to ignore. It would be Aunt Rosemary calling to renew the afternoon's attack, although how she could think of anything else to say he couldn't imagine. During the past week he'd heard every conceivable explanation for Alex's carelessness and all the evidence to support each one.

The ringing persisted, and Nick moved reluctantly toward the phone. If he didn't answer, she would only dial his grandfather and stir the embers of the argument Nick had spent most of the day trying to cool down.

Slumping into the sofa cushions, Nick raked tired fingers through his hair and then lifted the receiver from its cradle. A family-owned business, he thought. What a hell of a way to earn a living. "Yes?"

"Nick?"

It was Kylie's voice, husky and hesitant, and his weariness drained away beneath the soft pleasure washing over him. "Kylie." Just the taste of her name on his lips was satisfying, and he tried it again. "Kylie."

"Hi," she said. "How are you?"

His lips curved. "Lonely. How are you?"

"Sunburned and saturated with sight-seeing."

"And lonely?" he prodded gently.

"Yes, lonely."

The depth of feeling in her answer reassured him, and Nick ached with the need to touch her. "What did you do today?" he asked, trying to visualize the expression in her coffee-dark eyes.

"I washed my hair and let it dry while I napped in the sun. I read the newspaper, fifty pages of a dull novel, and the assertiveness training manual. I nibbled on leftovers and devoured all the junk food you had hidden in the cupboard." Her laugh came, low and lovely. "Are you thoroughly bored yet, or shall I continue this gripping narrative?"

"I'm thoroughly jealous. It must be nice to enjoy such nonvolatile activities. I'd trade my day for yours in the blink of an eye."

"Things aren't going well?" she asked in a sympathetic voice.

"Oh, we've progressed from obstinate, opinionated bias to a very loud silence that has now escalated into full-scale bargaining. But I'd say that a reasonable solution is still several days away."

"Oh." Disappointment sounded in her audible sigh. "How are you, Nick? *Really?*"

Her concern carried across the miles and soothed his

frustration. He needed this, he thought, needed her quiet comfort after the emotional tug-of-war he'd been through. "I'm fine, *really*. It's draining, but I'm used to this sort of family warfare. The situation will resolve itself, given time. It's just that I'd much prefer to spend the time with you. Sight-seeing and sunning and . . . so on."

"Especially so on." Her laughter sounded a little strained. "Actually all this inactivity is making me lazy. I've been thinking . . . " Her hesitation drew his brows into a frown. "Nick, I'm considering . . . Alex suggested that we . . . I mean, that I should resume the seminar as soon as possible . . . tomorrow, in fact."

The pause lasted just long enough for Nick to exhale a slow, cautious breath.

"Now, listen, before you start objecting," she continued in a rush, "the employees have been asking about the seminar. Alex thinks we've delayed long enough, and I have to agree. Nothing will go wrong, Nick, you'll see. Finishing the seminar now instead of later will be beneficial to the company and the employees."

He listened with a sense of detachment that surprised him. And when she paused again, obviously unsure of his reaction, Nick stared silently out the apartment window.

"Nick?" she questioned, her tone soft and appealing. "What . . . what do you think?"

"You know what I think, Kylie. Why bother to ask?"

"But you don't understand, Nick. The situation at Southwest is—"

"I think I understand perfectly." His voice, clipped and cool, sounded ominous even in his ears, and he knew with a fatalistic certainty that another argument was just a few words away. "The situation at Southwest is just as I left it—unsettled. You and Alex have put your heads together and come up with some nonsensical logic that will allow you to disregard my orders and do exactly as you please."

170

He heard her sharply indrawn breath, but still he made no move to stop the impending quarrel.

"That isn't fair, Nick. I'm trying to help. If you saw . . . if you were here . . . "

"You'd be doing the same thing, trying to change my mind by any means at your disposal. Maybe even a few indoor activities. Isn't that right, Kylie?"

"No! No, it isn't. You know I . . . "

The sentence ended with a choked cough, and Nick waited with deadly calm for her to regain her control. Damn! If he could get his hands on her right now, he'd make her forget that blasted seminar. But he couldn't touch her, couldn't even see her. And maybe that was just as well.

She was using him. And when this conversation was at an end, he knew his stomach was going to twist sickeningly with the knowledge. Kylie didn't care about him. She hadn't called because she wanted to talk to him, because she wanted to know how he was *really*. Sure, she said she was trying to help, but he didn't buy it for a minute. She wasn't concerned with anything except the fate of her precious seminar.

"Nick, please don't be so negative. This is important, and I want you to understand how I feel."

And what about how I feel, Kylie? The thought was in his mind, but he would not voice it. He would not let her know the hurt that snaked inside him, insidiously destroying his hopes for the future.

His grip on the phone tightened. "All right, Kylie. I understand. Is that what you want to hear? I understand that you want me to believe you're trying to help. Go ahead with your plans. Complete your seminar. I'm sure you and Alex will make it a resounding success. After all, my cousin is notorious for his good judgment and sound advice, isn't he? I can certainly understand why you'd want to follow his suggestions in preference to mine."

"Stop it," she said defiantly. "I know you don't mean that—"

"Ah, but you don't want to hear my real opinion, Kylie. You simply want the opportunity to tell me I'm wrong. The only reason you called tonight is that you were bored and needed someone to enliven your evening with an argument. And what a golden opportunity to polish up those assertiveness skills. Then, tomorrow, you can start the training session knowing that you applied every single principle in trying to reason with me."

"Damn it, Nick. Listen to me."

"I'm afraid I can't see the point, Kylie. I've already heard what you have to say. You don't have to go through it again. Have your seminar, with my blessing . . . as unimportant as that seems to be. Just don't expect me to come rushing to the rescue when the whole situation at the mill blows sky high. You'll have to put your trust in Alex because I wash my hands of you both."

"Good! Alex certainly doesn't need your kind of assistance, Nick. And as for me . . . well, I intend to salvage the employee-management relationship at Southwest just to prove to you that I can. You'll see that I don't need anyone to rescue me from this situation or any other."

"No, of course you don't. It was foolish of me to say such a ridiculous thing. I'd wish you luck, Kylie, but I'm sure you don't need that either. After all, fate wouldn't dare argue with you, would it?"

The receiver buzzed angrily in his ear, and Nick slowly replaced it. Then he laid his head against the sofa back and let the weariness settle over him again.

Kylie commanded her hand to stop trembling as finger by finger she released her death grip on the telephone.

How could he say those things to her? How could he even think such things?

Her heart pounded rapidly against her rib cage, but she couldn't pinpoint the cause. Hurt and anger were so closely intermingled inside her that she couldn't separate them. At first she thought the aching hurt would win out and engulf her, but she drew a deliberate breath and focused on her anger. No matter how she felt about him, Nick had no right to speak to her that way. He was stubborn and opinionated, and he would never, never be able to admit he was wrong. She had been incredibly naïve to think there was ever a chance of winning his respect for her professionally.

With wide-eyed innocence she had given him her heart, put her faith in happy endings, and all she had to show for it was empty arms. Nick wanted someone pliable and yielding. He didn't want a relationship of mutual respect and responsibility. And any man who had to be in charge of every situation was no prize . . . not for her, at any rate.

There was little she could do to rescue her heart at this point, but she would have the satisfaction of proving him wrong about the seminar, proving that she had helped him whether he wanted to believe it or not. She would show him or die trying.

The next morning Southwest Textiles employees were going to receive a stimulating lecture on positive self-motivation. No matter that the topic would be aimed at her own faltering resolve. And no matter that her enthusiasm would be largely manufactured by the very self-control theories she taught.

All the more reason to put her best efforts into these last sessions. The seminar would be a success—an undeniable success. She wouldn't allow her self-confidence to be shaken by Nick's subtle take-over of her emotions.

It was a reasonable goal to set, she decided firmly. A

goal she could strive for and obtain and one that offered a full measure of satisfaction.

And for now that would be enough, Kylie warned her willful heart. It would be enough.

CHAPTER TEN

Satisfaction was a relative term, Kylie decided during the
busy days and weeks that followed. The completion of the
seminar brought not only a measure of satisfaction but
also a much-needed reinforcement of her self-confidence.
Notwithstanding Nick's belief that everything would blow
sky high at the mill under her leadership, the last sessions
of the seminar alleviated the tension of an explosive situation and restored calm at Southwest.

And it was certainly satisfying on her return to San
Diego to begin a management development course at a
local department store. Without a doubt the quarterly
production report from Southwest Textiles that now lay
on her desk and the pale-blue wedding invitation that had
accompanied the report were sources of sweet satisfaction.

Alex and Stephanie had resolved their differences and
discovered each other as a result of the training seminar.
They had said so themselves, and surely that was reason
for satisfaction. Alex had faced the problems at Southwest
and had made a trip to the home office to request another

chance. A request that obviously had been granted. That in itself was satisfying. Wasn't it?

Kylie frowned at the view from her office window. The Pacific Ocean etched the horizon with majestic white-capped waves somewhere beyond her range of vision. And likewise beautiful San Diego Bay rippled peacefully just out of sight. She couldn't enjoy either because of the brick-and-mortar office buildings that stretched intrusively between her window and the water. And she couldn't enjoy a well-deserved sense of accomplishment because of the intrusive dissatisfaction that filled her.

Stubborn, she concluded dismally. If Nick wasn't so stubborn, she would be feeling excessively pleased with herself right now. And she wouldn't be spending so much time staring out the window at a very empty view.

Kylie turned to look at the papers clipped neatly to the file folder marked Southwest Textiles, Inc. The production report showed an unquestionable improvement—one that even Nick, as stubborn as he was, couldn't deny. At least she didn't believe he would deny it . . . if she ever saw him again, which at the moment seemed a very remote possibility.

Kylie walked to the desk and ran a well-manicured fingertip down the columns of the report. Vindication, she thought dryly, lost its punch without a cheering section.

There had been more than enough time for Nick to analyze the figures. He could have written a note of thanks for her part in defusing the flare-up at the mill. Or he could have written a note of apology, admitting that he'd been wrong. He could have written "Congratulations" or "It was nice knowing you" or even "Let's agree to disagree one more time." But it was becoming blatantly obvious that he had no intention of writing anything. He hadn't recognized the value of her way of thinking, and he hadn't seen the value in her. He hadn't even said good-bye.

She tapped an ambiguous rhythm against the desk. It wasn't fair. Nick at least owed her the acknowledgment of a job well done. And after all that had happened, she deserved the satisfaction of throwing the report in his face and saying, "I told you so." It would be a wonderful release of tension . . . and besides it was the only excuse for seeing him that had occurred to her so far.

Although Kylie hated to admit she needed an excuse, she couldn't deny that she wanted to see him, needed to see him. And she was afraid that courage would never take her as far as the door of her own office, much less Nick's.

Before determination gave way to doubt, she made a reservation on the next flight to San Francisco. It took only two phone calls to rearrange her schedule for the rest of the day and only a little over an hour to pack an overnight case.

When she finally sank into the aisle seat and felt the plane's engines humming in readiness for takeoff, Kylie wondered if she had taken leave of her senses. But the jerky movement of the airplane canceled any thoughts of forgetting the whole idea. For better or worse she was going to San Francisco, and since she would be in town anyway, she might as well drop in to see Nick.

During the flight Kylie examined that casual line from several angles and knew she was wasting her time. Nick would see through any excuse she concocted. He would know why she'd come, and perhaps that was just as well since she wasn't quite sure what she expected to gain from seeing him again. What would she . . . what could she say to him?

She carefully prepared a dignified speech and rehearsed it on the taxi ride from the airport. It even sounded almost natural by the time she entered the office building. But when she followed a politely smiling secretary into Nick's office, Kylie knew no amount of rehearsal would have made any difference.

She was aware of the afternoon sunlight streaming through windows that promised a stunning view, she saw the dark wood bookshelves, noticed the modernistic furnishings, felt the rich carpeting beneath her feet. She even registered the curious stares of the two women who stood quietly beside Nick.

But Nick was the focal point of her attention. He seemed taller, more attractive than she remembered. His hair appeared darker, longer, and his facial features showed lines of strain. The appealing cleft in his chin was noticeably absent. The curve of his lips missed being a smile, and he looked at her questioningly.

For a moment lost in time Kylie met his gaze and felt her senses reel at the sight of him. Everything else diminished in importance, and she was suddenly, inexplicably complete.

"Hello, Nick," she said as casually as if her heart weren't pounding madly. "How have you been? I was in the neighborhood and thought I'd drop by to discuss the production report from Southwest. I'm sure you'll remember my prediction of an increase—"

"Hello, Kylie," he interrupted with no hint of emotion. "May I introduce you to my mother and my aunt?"

Swallowing her impulsive need to talk, Kylie snapped her manners into place and stepped forward. She acknowledged the introductions with a courteous smile, feeling slightly uncomfortable under Nick's intent gaze. Did he think she was going to make some horrible social blunder or something?

"It's so nice to meet you," she murmured with a polite cordiality that within moments warmed to sincerity. Gray eyes, so like Nick's, welcomed her. Jane Braden McKaye was like her son in other ways too. Her sable-dark hair was

178

misted with silver, and the latent amusement in her eyes and in her smile was softer, but even so she reminded Kylie of Nick. Her charm was quiet and unpretentious, dispelling Kylie's reticence with its patience.

Aunt Rosemary's charm, on the other hand, demanded an immediate response. Her blond vivaciousness was both compelling and a little overpowering. In the second it took the speculating blue eyes to assess her, Kylie felt she'd been weighed, measured, and checked for cavities. Still, if Nick hadn't forewarned her about his aunt, Kylie doubted that she would have recognized the thoroughness of the survey; it had been handled with such finesse.

"Please sit down, Kylie." Mrs. McKaye assumed the role of hostess and motioned Kylie to a leather-upholstered chair. "Nick has been so mysterious about you that we must have a chance to get acquainted. Men can be so frustratingly closemouthed at times, you know."

Kylie glanced at Nick for reassurance or guidance or some equally vague assistance, but he didn't acknowledge her request. He just perched on the edge of the sizable desk, folded his arms over his chest, and watched her with expressionless serenity.

"Yes." Kylie tried the affirmative answer, hoping it would fit somewhere. Sinking into the rich leather, she attempted a nonchalant smile as Rosemary Jamison circled the chair to sit opposite her.

"So you're Kylie." The statement was delivered with such a knowing look that Kylie wondered just how closemouthed Nick had actually been. Her gaze strayed helplessly in his direction but, finding no response, returned to his aunt.

The stylish hairstyle didn't alter by a single blond strand as Rosemary gave a discerning nod. "You're Kylie," she repeated as if confirming a suspicion. "You really made quite an impression on my son, Alex. But then,

179

apparently you made quite an impression on . . . everyone."

Kylie felt compelled to glance at the "everyone" in question and thought that he didn't appear very impressed. "I'm afraid that's a little exaggerated," she said with a determined sigh. "Even at the end of the seminar there were a few holdouts. Some people just can't seem to focus on the positive aspects of life."

"Thick heads, no doubt," Nick's mother inserted blandly.

Kylie blinked in surprise at the benign humor and resisted the urge to agree aloud. Instead she lifted her shoulders in a slight shrug. "I've been told that differences of opinion add zest to life."

"Only if you define zest as bickering, quibbling, and a general state of dissension," Rosemary said, reclaiming Kylie's attention with an almost disarming laugh. "Personally I can't understand why anyone's opinion would differ from mine."

Although she felt sure Rosemary was only joking, Kylie wasn't sure how to respond. With a mental flip of a coin she chose a light comment. "I sometimes feel the same way, but luckily I'm wrong often enough to keep me humble."

"And right often enough to keep you confident," Jane McKaye added with a hint of admiration. "I understand you can be very assertive."

Kylie curbed the inclination to check Nick's reaction. "I like to think I'm capable of responding appropriately, whether the situation calls for assertiveness or deference to another's opinion."

Rosemary arched a thoughtful eyebrow. "Tell me about these seminars you give, Kylie."

This time Kylie couldn't keep her gaze from Nick. Was he never going to say anything? What was he thinking as she sat here chatting aimlessly? His expression told her nothing, yet she could sense his thoughts, his feelings reaching toward her.

Her hand trembled with the need to touch him, to share her uncertainty and to receive his reassurance. She was here in his office because she loved him, would always love him, and she couldn't sit casually discussing something as mundane as a seminar. Not now.

She felt the curious stares of the other women as she looked at him, desire etched deeply in her face. Nick's eyes never left her face. Longing laced a path to her fingertips, but she dared not move to go to him.

Nick closed his eyes, and for one devastating second Kylie thought he was going to get up and leave the room, but slowly his lashes lifted, and she saw the emotion, her own emotions, mirrored in his gaze.

"Mother, Aunt Rosemary," he said as he stood and walked to where she was sitting. He raised her slowly from the chair. "If you'll excuse us, Kylie and I have some things to . . . talk about."

Nick, holding her arm, propelled her toward the door. They were halfway there before Kylie heard Mrs. McKaye's tentative "It was nice to meet you." And they were halfway through the reception area before Kylie gave up on trying to force a reply past the lump in her throat.

She wondered where Nick was taking her and when he would finally say something, anything. But even when they were alone in the elevator, he was silent.

Kylie maintained the distance of a few inches that Nick had established between them and eyed him with uncertainty. "I'm beginning to think your mother is right," she said. "You're being frustratingly closemouthed."

He turned, and the cleft in his chin made an unexpected appearance. "Kylie, right now I don't know whether to wring your neck or kiss you breathless."

Her hesitation was only momentary. "I've always found the positive approach to be the best."

"Really? And which approach do you consider positive? Wringing your neck or kissing you breathless?"

Venting the full force of her frown on him, she lifted her chin. "If that's the way you're going to be . . . "

His hand cupped her chin and tilted it up even more. "This is the way I'd like to be . . . " The words fanned her cheeks in the instant before his mouth laid claim to hers. Kylie wilted against him, lost, at last, in his kiss.

But just as his arms curved around her, the elevator swooped to a stop, and Nick stepped back.

"I'm not breathless yet," she said with a fragile smile.

"Give me a chance, Kylie." He reached for her hand as the elevator doors opened. "This isn't the ideal spot for a thorough demonstration."

"Do you know someplace better?"

"Much better."

She glanced at him as they walked from the building into the fading sunlight. "Is it private?" she asked provocatively. "I mean, there aren't any live-in blondes or anything like that?"

"Only if you count the cocker spaniel who lives next door."

Kylie wanted to laugh aloud with the giddy wonder of loving him. She was with Nick again, and everything was going to be all right.

When he held open the taxi door, she slid across the seat to make room for him and then suddenly remembered. "Nick, my purse . . . I left it in your office."

He slammed the door and nodded to the driver. "You won't need it. We'll get it later."

"But my overnight case and the briefcase with the production report—"

"You won't be needing either one."

"I might." Her voice lacked both concern and conviction as she looked into his eyes and arched a teasing eyebrow. "I *know* you'll want to discuss the report with me."

His hand slipped warningly around her nape. "I've changed my mind. I'm going to kiss you until you're speechless."

Her lips slanted in a saucy smile. "If you think you can . . ."

Nick accepted the challenge without hesitation, and by the time the taxi pulled to a stop, Kylie had long since conceded defeat. She had neither the will nor the desire to speak as she accompanied Nick into the two-story brick building. His apartment was at the top of a graceful stairway, and Kylie entertained fanciful thoughts of floating up the steps and into his arms every day for the rest of her life.

Inside, his apartment was neat, modern, and crisply masculine. But she had little time for observation. Nick closed the door, turned the lock with a definite click, and drew her to him. His hands held her provocatively against the hard muscles of his thighs. "Now that we're alone, why don't you tell me why you're here?"

Kylie had no intention of teasing, of being coy, of waiting to hear a declaration of love before admitting that she cared. She wanted to tell Nick all that she felt, and she no longer had any fear that he would reject her love. He loved her too. She knew it with every beat of her heart. But, caught somewhere between the duskiness of his eyes and the sweet desires that held her hostage, she couldn't speak.

The words of love filled her, rising and thickening inside her with the need to be expressed. Such simple words, but so achingly, beautifully complex when coupled with the emotion that gave them voice. And still she stood silent, letting the words abide in her eyes, placing her trembling finger against his lips to convey the depth of her love. Then she slipped free of her sandals to raise herself on tiptoe and lift her face to his. She brushed the corner of his mouth with the promise of a kiss.

"Nick, oh, Nick." She whispered his name until at last emotion broke the bonds of silence. "I love you." It felt so good, sounded so wonderful that she smiled and said it again. "Oh, Nick, I love you."

His arms tightened around her, and the same hesitancy she'd experienced only a moment before now echoed in his eyes. But Kylie waited, knowing that when he spoke, the words would be rich with feeling.

"I love you," he murmured huskily, and then he shifted to swing her into his arms. Cradling her to his chest, Nick locked her in his gaze. "I thought I was imagining things when I saw you walk into the office today. And then I decided that you'd only come to taunt me with that production report."

"Well, I . . . " Kylie began tentatively. "It was a good excuse for coming, and I would like to know that you at least looked at the report and what you thought about it. Even if you won't admit that I was right or that I did help you."

His eyes spoke a rueful apology. "I looked at the report. I thought it was a very convincing argument. I admit you were right in your assessment of the situation at Southwest. You did help. We'll go over it item by item, if you like—later. Right now we have better things to do." He started toward the bedroom, his arms firm and tender beneath her, his voice a soothing accompaniment to his strides. "Until today, Kylie, I didn't realize why I fell in love with you so quickly and so completely.

"From the moment I first saw you in the airport, I knew there was something special, something different about you. But today, watching you with Mother and Aunt

Rosemary, it occurred to me that you possess the qualities I most admire in them. You're strong and independent, and yet you're still sensitive and vulnerable. I've never before found that combination in a woman."

As he lowered her onto the bed Nick caressed her cheek with the back of his hand. "And now you're here with me." His sigh revealed the strain of the days they'd spent apart. "I convinced myself you really didn't care for me. It seemed like you were fighting me, arguing with me at every turn. That day on the telephone when you kept repeating Alex's name, telling me what he said, how he felt—"

"I only wanted you to understand, Nick."

"And I misunderstood entirely. I just couldn't believe the seminar could be as effective as you said. But you proved its value, and you deserve the credit for resolving a touchy situation." He shrugged free of his jacket, tossed it aside, and lay beside her. "God, I've missed you, Kylie. You don't know how—"

"Show me," she whispered, curving her arms around his neck and pressing into his embrace. "Please, Nick, show me."

It was a scene Kylie had envisioned many times during the long empty nights without him. A moment she had feared would never be hers. Yet now that she was here, her body warmed by his and her heart beating in rhythm with his, she could hardly believe it was happening. It was too perfect, too precious to be real.

But as piece by piece the mound of discarded clothing on the floor grew, her lips and her fingertips explored the reality that was Nick. And he rediscovered her in a myriad of ways, touching, stroking, and searing her skin with dozens of tiny, sipping kisses.

His mouth at her breast gave her intense pleasure, and she felt his satisfaction as her hands remembered the ways to please him. She rubbed her foot along his hair-roughened leg and delighted in his response. Their lips met, parted, and met again in long, yearning kisses that transcended the moment and soared into eternity.

The hunger to feel his possession throbbed within her, and Kylie arched her body into his, seeking to give and receive a sweet fulfillment.

Passion flared in fiery waves, but for all the urgency of their union Kylie felt the same lingering seduction of her senses, the completeness that she knew belonged uniquely to her and Nick.

The satisfaction remained long after the storm of their desire had spent itself. Kylie lay content, wrapped in his embrace, too bemused with loving him to do more than sigh occasionally.

Nick rubbed her shoulder in slow, soothing strokes. "Now that you're here, Kylie, I intend to keep you." His breath warmed her temple, and she closed her eyes to savor the wispy touch. "You know that, don't you?" he asked. "I don't want any arguments about it. We'll plan a wedding during the Christmas holidays. That will give you plenty of time to relocate—"

"Wait, Nick," she protested, turning to look at him. "I thought I just heard you mention a wedding . . . next Christmas?"

"Well, I think it should be a long engagement. You will marry me, won't you?"

"Yes, Nick, of course I will, but what is the point of an engagement, long or otherwise?"

"We're going to need time to relocate your company in San Francisco. This will be a good opportunity for you, Kylie. Your business is bound to benefit by a move north. I have a lot of contacts here, and now that you've proved the effectiveness of your seminar, I should be able to talk some of those aging, autocratic idiots you're so fond of into listening to your seminar presentations."

Kylie kept very still, listening to his careful plans. They were solid plans, wonderful plans for the future that she could agree with completely . . . except for one tiny detail.

Her sigh sailed past lips frozen in a frown. "Nick, did you ever once consider asking what I thought about all this? It might not be feasible to move my business at the moment. I might not want to wait until Christmas to be married. I might have plans and commitments of my own to consider. Couldn't you ask me before you start making decisions that affect both of us?"

His breathing slowed, and she felt caution flood through him. The moment lengthened into a weighty silence as Nick increased the pressure of his embrace and then released it. "I think, Kylie, that I'm afraid to ask."

For all the steadiness in his voice she heard the uncertainty, recognized his unspoken need for reassurance. "Nick, I love you. I need you. You're a part of my life now. I couldn't make any plans that didn't include you if I tried. It's just that I want to be, insist on being, an equal partner in our relationship. I can't settle for less than that."

"I want that too," he agreed huskily. "I'm just not at all sure how to go about establishing equality. I know I'm stubborn at times . . . " He paused to wrap her in a smile. "Not as stubborn as you are, but stubborn just the same. I want to give you so much, Kylie. I want to protect you and love you. I want to be needed by you." He inhaled a low deep breath. "We're both strong willed. Do you think we can make our marriage a success? I want a long-term commitment, Kylie. I won't settle for less."

Turning onto her side, Kylie braced herself against his chest and planted a confident kiss squarely on his lips. "I've always had a firm belief in positive thinking, and I'd

187

be happy to give you some individual instruction. Could I interest you in private lessons?"

"If you're willing to put up with my occasional relapses into taking charge of your life, I think we should begin the lessons at once. But I warn you that it may take years for me to get the hang of it."

"I'm not worried," she assured him solemnly. "You'll have a lifetime to practice."

His arms curved invitingly, pulling her close and allowing his lips access to the delightful hollows of her shoulder. "And a lifetime to practice other equally important activities. Perhaps I might interest you in a different type of lesson?"

"Mmmm, I don't know." She savored the seductive heat of his kisses. "I'd have to know exactly what kind of lesson you have in mind."

"Forget I asked. This is one time you'll just have to accept my decision as final." He sealed the command with a tender tasting of her lips.

Kylie drew back and smiled into his love-darkened eyes. "I don't intend to let it become a habit, but just this one time I will lovingly acquiesce to your wishes."

"Thank God, I was afraid you were going to argue."

"I love you, Nick," she whispered. "How could I possibly argue with that?"

"I adore a woman who knows her own mind."

Her lips formed a curve of surrender. "And I'm fascinated by an assertive man. Isn't it lucky we found each other?"

"Luck had nothing to do with it," he said with a slow, nuzzling caress along her neck. "It was the power of positive thinking."

"Yes, of course," Kylie agreed dreamily. "How could it be anything else?"

LOOK FOR NEXT MONTH'S
CANDLELIGHT ECSTASY ROMANCES ®

Candlelight

Ecstasy Romances™

$1.95 each

$2.50 each

At your local bookstore or use this handy coupon for ordering:

Dell DELL BOOKS   B109B
P.O. BOX 1000. PINE BROOK. N.J. 07058-1000

Please send me the books I have checked above. I am enclosing $ _____ (please add 75c per copy to cover postage and handling). Send check or money order—no cash or C.O.D.'s. Please allow up to 8 weeks for shipment.

Name _____

Address _____

City _____ State Zip _____

Breathtaking sagas of adventure and romance

VALERIE VAYLE